SHORT STORIES

E

*for the London Association
for the Teaching of English by*

DOUGLAS R. BARNES, M.A.

*Formerly Senior English Master
Minchenden Grammar School*

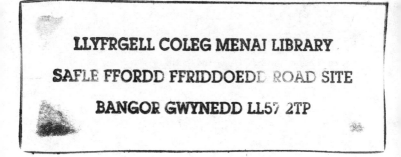
Nelson

Thomas Nelson and Sons Ltd
Nelson House   Mayfield Road
Walton-on-Thames   Surrey
KT12 5PL   UK

51 York Place
Edinburgh
EH1 3JD   UK

Thomas Nelson (Hong Kong) Ltd
Toppan Building 10/F
22A Westlands Road
Quarry Bay   Hong Kong

Thomas Nelson Australia
102 Dodds Street
South Melbourne
Victoria 3205   Australia

Nelson Canada
1120 Birchmount Road
Scarborough   Ontario
M1K 5G4   Canada

First published by George C Harrap and Co Ltd 1963
(under ISBN 0-245-52994-2)
Reprinted 27 times

Twenty eighth impression published by Thomas Nelson and Sons Ltd 1984

ISBN 0-17-445094-X
NPN 19 18 17 16 15 14 13

Printed in Hong Kong.

PREFACE

THESE stories are chosen because pupils enjoy reading them. 'Enjoyment', however, does not here mean relaxation into the pleasant vaguenesses of a fantasy world, where dreams effortlessly consummate themselves. The stories will give more according to the attention they receive.

When boys and girls scornfully say that 'the classics' are about nothing they may well be telling a relative truth. To respond to the human meaning of a story concerning people and manners alien to the reader is a sophisticated activity that many adults find difficult. Thus a Dickens novel, quite apart from the difficulty of the language, may communicate little to a young reader. Most of the stories in this book are set firmly in a twentieth-century urban milieu, and they deal with aspects of the life that is confronting their young readers—the meaning of education in *The First Seven Years*, political protest in *The Raid*, their attitude to elderly people in *A Present for a Good Girl* and *Life of Ma Parker*, and the power of the Press in *Shot Actress—Full Story*.

As the stories concern ordinary people in realistic situations, they offer many opportunities for the kind of discussion that moves out from the text into life. For instance, to discuss *Possessions* without tapping pupils' recollections of their own families' dearest possessions would be to deprive them of much of the story's potential meaning. To the academic literary critic such discussion may seem irrelevant, but for the teacher this provides the most rewarding way of helping his pupils to give body to the words of the story, to re-create it out of their own experience. After such discussion the pupils return to the story with a fuller awareness of its relevance to them and of its relationship with the reality that they know.

At the end of this volume are sets of questions on all of the stories: they are intended not to provide opportunities for written work but to lead the pupil into the story and to help direct discussion in class. The questions avoid the abstractions of literary criticism and are intended to help pupils to look more closely at what the story is and does. When it seems appropriate the questions ask the pupils to make connections between the story and the reality that they know, though many other opportunities for this will occur to teachers.

The editors have tried in this selection to envisage the needs of fourth form, fifth form, and older pupils in any kind of secondary school who will study enthusiastically only works that they feel to be immediately relevant.

D.R.B.

ACKNOWLEDGMENTS

THIS book has been edited for the London Association for the Teaching of English by Margaret Tucker of Mayfield County School, Catherine Dowling of Maria Assumpta Training College, Patricia Myers of Holland Park Comprehensive School, and Douglas R. Barnes of Minchenden Grammar School. These editors would like to express gratitude to all other teachers who have given advice and suggestions.

Thanks are due to the following for permission to include stories in this collection:

Mr Bernard Malamud and Messrs Eyre & Spottiswoode, Ltd, for *The First Seven Years*, from *The Magic Barrel*; Mr H. E. Bates and Messrs Jonathan Cape, Ltd, for *Shot Actress—Full Story*, from *Twenty Tales*; Mr Dan Jacobson and Messrs Weidenfeld and Nicholson, Ltd, for *The Little Pet*, from *A Long Way from London*; The Society of Authors as the literary representative of the Estate of the late Katherine Mansfield and Messrs Constable and Co., Ltd, for *Life of Ma Parker*, from *The Garden Party*; Mr John Wain and Messrs Macmillan and Co., Ltd, for *A Message from the Pig-Man*, from *Nuncle*; Mr Irwin Shaw and Messrs Jonathan Cape, Ltd, for *The Dry Rock*, from *Mixed Company*; Miss Doris Lessing and Messrs MacGibbon and Kee, Ltd, for *Through the Tunnel*, from *The Habit of Loving*; Miss Nadine Gordimer and Messrs Victor Gollancz, Ltd, for *A Present for a Good Girl*, from *The Soft Voice of the Serpent*; Mr G. Ewart Evans, for *Possessions*; Mr John Steinbeck and Messrs

William Heinemann, Ltd, for *The Raid*, from *The Long Valley*; Miss Mary Lavin and Messrs Macmillan and Co., Ltd, for *The Living*, from *Winter's Tales*; Mr Alan Sillitoe and W. H. Allen and Co., for *Uncle Ernest*, from *The Loneliness of the Long Distance Runner*; Mr Bill Naughton and Messrs MacGibbon and Kee, Ltd, for *Late Night on Watling Street*, from *Late Night on Watling Street*.

CONTENTS

BERNARD MALAMUD

The First Seven Years

FELD, the shoemaker, was annoyed that his helper, Sobel,
was so insensitive to his reverie that he wouldn't for a
minute cease his fanatic pounding at the other bench. He
gave him a look, but Sobel's bald head was bent over the
last as he worked and he didn't notice. The shoemaker
shrugged and continued to peer through the partly frosted
window at the near-sighted haze of falling February snow.
Neither the shifting white blur outside nor the sudden deep
remembrance of the snowy Polish village where he had
wasted his youth could turn his thoughts from Max the
college boy (a constant visitor in the mind since early that
morning when Feld saw him trudging through the snow-
drifts on his way to school), whom he so much respected
because of the sacrifices he had made throughout the years—
in winter or direst heat—to further his education. An old
wish returned to haunt the shoemaker: that he had had a son
instead of a daughter, but this blew away in the snow for
Feld, if anything, was a practical man. Yet he could not help
but contrast the diligence of the boy, who was a pedlar's
son, with Miriam's unconcern for an education. True, she
was always with a book in her hand, yet when the opportunity arose for a college education, she had said no she

would rather find a job. He had begged her to go, pointing out how many fathers could not afford to send their children to college, but she said she wanted to be independent. As for education, what was it, she asked, but books, which Sobel, who diligently read the classics, would as usual advise her on. Her answer greatly grieved her father.

A figure emerged from the snow and the door opened. At the counter the man withdrew from a wet paper bag a pair of battered shoes for repair. Who he was the shoemaker for a moment had no idea, then his heart trembled as he realized, before he had thoroughly discerned the face, that Max himself was standing there, embarrassedly explaining what he wanted done to his old shoes. Though Feld listened eagerly, he couldn't hear a word, for the opportunity that had burst upon him was deafening.

He couldn't exactly recall when the thought had occurred to him, because it was clear he had more than once considered suggesting to the boy that he go out with Miriam. But he had not dared speak, for if Max said no, how would he face him again? Or suppose Miriam, who harped so often on independence, blew up in anger and shouted at him for his meddling? Still, the chance was too good to let by: all it meant was an introduction. They might long ago have become friends had they happened to meet somewhere, therefore was it not his duty—an obligation—to bring them together, nothing more, a harmless connivance to replace an accidental encounter in the subway, let's say, or a mutual friend's introduction in the street? Just let him once see and talk to her and he would for sure be interested. As for Miriam, what possible harm for a working girl in an office, who met only loud-mouthed salesmen and illiterate shipping

clerks, to make the acquaintance of a fine scholarly boy?
Maybe he would awaken in her a desire to go to college; if
not—the shoemaker's mind at last came to grips with the
truth—let her marry an educated man and live a better life.

When Max finished describing what he wanted done to
his shoes, Feld marked them, both with enormous holes in
the soles which he pretended not to notice, with large white-
chalk x's, and the rubber heels, thinned to the nails, he
marked with o's, though it troubled him he might have mixed
up the letters. Max inquired the price, and the shoemaker
cleared his throat and asked the boy, above Sobel's insistent
hammering, would he please step through the side door
there into the hall. Though surprised, Max did as the shoemaker requested, and Feld went in after him. For a minute
they were both silent, because Sobel had stopped banging,
and it seemed they understood neither was to say anything
until the noise began again. When it did, loudly, the shoemaker quickly told Max why he had asked to talk to him.

'Ever since you went to high school,' he said, in the
dimly lit hallway, 'I watched you in the morning go to the
subway to school, and I said always to myself, this is a fine
boy that he wants so much an education.'

'Thanks,' Max said, nervously alert. He was tall and
grotesquely thin, with sharply cut features, particularly a
beak-like nose. He was wearing a loose, long slushy overcoat that hung down to his ankles, looking like a rug draped
over his bony shoulders, and a soggy, old brown hat, as
battered as the shoes he had brought in.

'I am a business man,' the shoemaker abruptly said to
conceal his embarrassment, 'so I will explain you right away
why I talk to you. I have a girl, my daughter Miriam—she is

nineteen—a very nice girl and also so pretty that everybody looks on her when she passes by in the street. She is smart, always with a book, and I thought to myself that a boy like you, an educated boy—I thought maybe you will be interested sometime to meet a girl like this.' He laughed a bit when he had finished and was tempted to say more but had the good sense not to.

Max stared down like a hawk. For an uncomfortable second he was silent, then he asked, 'Did you say nineteen?'

'Yes.'

'Would it be all right to enquire if you have a picture of her?'

'Just a minute.' The shoemaker went into the store and hastily returned with a snapshot that Max held up to the light.

'She's all right,' he said.

Feld waited.

'And is she sensible—not the flighty kind?'

'She is very sensible.'

After another short pause, Max said it was okay with him if he met her.

'Here is my telephone,' said the shoemaker, hurriedly handing him a slip of paper. 'Call her up. She comes home from work six o'clock.'

Max folded the paper and tucked it away into his worn leather wallet.

'About the shoes,' he said. 'How much did you say they cost me?'

'Don't worry about the price.'

'I just like to have an idea.'

'A dollar—dollar fifty. A dollar fifty,' the shoemaker said. At once he felt bad, for he usually charged two twenty-five for this kind of job. Either he should have asked the regular price or done the work for nothing.

Later, as he entered the store, he was startled by a violent clanging and looked up to see Sobel pounding with all his might upon the naked last. It broke, the iron striking the floor and jumping with a thump against the wall, but before the enraged shoemaker could cry out, the assistant had torn his hat and coat from the hook and rushed out into the snow.

★

So Feld, who had looked forward to anticipating how it would go with his daughter and Max, instead had a great worry on his mind. Without his temperamental helper he was a lost man, especially since it was years now that he had carried the store alone. The shoemaker had for an age suffered from a heart condition that threatened collapse if he dared exert himself. Five years ago, after an attack, it had appeared as though he would have either to sacrifice his business upon the auction block and live on a pittance thereafter, or put himself at the mercy of some unscrupulous employee who would in the end probably ruin him. But just at the moment of his darkest despair, this Polish refugee, Sobel, appeared one night from the street and begged for work. He was a stocky man, poorly dressed, with a bald head that had once been blond, a severely plain face and soft blue eyes prone to tears over the sad books he read, a young man but old—no one would have guessed thirty. Though he confessed he knew nothing of shoemaking, he said he was apt and would work for a very little if Feld taught him the trade. Thinking that with, after all, a landsman he would have less to fear than from a complete stranger, Feld took him on and within six weeks the refugee rebuilt as good a shoe as he, and not long thereafter expertly ran the business for the thoroughly relieved shoemaker.

Feld could trust him with anything and did, frequently going home after an hour or two at the store, leaving all the money in the till, knowing Sobel would guard every cent of it. The amazing thing was that he demanded so little. His wants were few; in money he wasn't interested —in nothing but books, it seemed—which he one by one lent to Miriam, together with his profuse, queer written comments, manufactured during his lonely rooming house evenings, thick pads of commentary which the shoemaker peered at and twitched his shoulders over as his daughter, from her fourteenth year, read page by sanctified page, as if the word of God were inscribed on them. To protect Sobel, Feld himself had to see that he received more than he asked for. Yet his conscience bothered him for not in- sisting that the assistant accept a better wage than he was getting, though Feld had honestly told him he could earn a handsome salary if he worked elsewhere, or maybe opened a place of his own. But the assistant answered, somewhat ungraciously, that he was not interested in going elsewhere, and though Feld frequently asked himself what keeps him here? why does he stay? he finally answered it that the man, no doubt because of his terrible experiences as a refugee, was afraid of the world.

After the incident with the broken last, angered by Sobel's behaviour, the shoemaker decided to let him stew for a week in the rooming house, although his own strength was taxed dangerously and the business suffered. However, after several sharp nagging warnings from both his wife and daughter, he went finally in search of Sobel, as he had

once before, quite recently, when over some fancied slight
—Feld had merely asked him not to give Miriam so many
books to read because her eyes were strained and red—the
assistant had left the place in a huff, an incident which, as
usual, came to nothing for he had returned after the shoemaker had talked to him, and taken his seat at the bench.
But this time, after Feld had plodded through the snow to
Sobel's house—he had thought of sending Miriam but the
idea became repugnant to him—the burly landlady at the
door informed him in a nasal voice that Sobel was not at
home, and though Feld knew this was a nasty lie, for where
had the refugee to go? still for some reason he was not completely sure of—it may have been the cold and his fatigue
—he decided not to insist on seeing him. Instead he went
home and hired a new helper.

That settled the matter, though not entirely to his
satisfaction, for he had much more to do than before, and
so, for example, could no longer lie late in bed mornings
because he had to get up to open the store for the new
assistant, a speechless, dark man with an irritating rasp as
he worked, whom he would not trust with the key as he
had Sobel. Furthermore, this one, though able to do a fair
repair job, knew nothing of grades of leather or prices, so
Feld had to make his own purchases; and every night at
closing time it was necessary to count the money in the till
and lock up. However, he was not dissatisfied, for he lived
much in his thoughts of Max and Miriam. The college boy
had called her, and they had arranged a meeting for this
coming Friday night. The shoemaker would personally
have preferred Saturday, which he felt would make it a
date of the first magnitude, but he learned Friday was

Miriam's choice, so he said nothing. The day of the week did not matter. What mattered was the aftermath. Would they like each other and want to be friends? He sighed at all the time that would have to go by before he knew for sure. Often he was tempted to talk to Miriam about the boy, to ask whether she thought she would like his type—he had told her only that he considered Max a nice boy and had suggested he call her—but the one time he tried she snapped at him—justly—how should she know?

At last Friday came. Feld was not feeling particularly well so he stayed in bed, and Mrs Feld thought it better to remain in the bedroom with him when Max called. Miriam received the boy, and her parents could hear their voices, his throaty one, as they talked. Just before leaving, Miriam brought Max to the bedroom door and he stood there a minute, a tall, slightly hunched figure wearing a thick, droopy suit, and apparently at ease as he greeted the shoemaker and his wife, which was surely a good sign. And Miriam, although she had worked all day, looked fresh and pretty. She was a large-framed girl with a well-shaped body, and she had a fine open face and soft hair. They made, Feld thought, a first-class couple.

Miriam returned after 11.30. Her mother was already asleep, but the shoemaker got out of bed and after locating his bathrobe went into the kitchen, where Miriam, to his surprise, sat at the table, reading.

'So where did you go?' Feld asked pleasantly.

'For a walk,' she said, not looking up.

'I advised him,' Feld said, clearing his throat, 'he shouldn't spend so much money.'

'I didn't care.'

The shoemaker boiled up some water for tea and sat down at the table with a cupful and a thick slice of lemon.

'So how,' he sighed after a sip, 'did you enjoy?'

'It was all right.'

He was silent. She must have sensed his disappointment, for she added, 'You can't really tell much the first time.'

'You will see him again?'

Turning a page, she said that Max had asked for another date.

'For when?'

'Saturday.'

'So what did you say?'

'What did I say?' she asked, delaying for a moment—'I said yes.'

Afterwards she inquired about Sobel, and Feld, without exactly knowing why, said the assistant had got another job. Miriam said nothing more and began to read. The shoemaker's conscience did not trouble him; he was satisfied with the Saturday date.

During the week, by placing here and there a deft question, he managed to get from Miriam some information about Max. It surprised him to learn that the boy was not studying to be either a doctor or lawyer but was taking a business course leading to a degree in accountancy. Feld was a little disappointed because he thought of accountants as book-keepers and would have preferred a 'higher profession'. However, it was not long before he had investigated the subject and discovered that Certified Public Accountants were highly respected people, so he was thoroughly content as Saturday approached. But because Saturday was a busy day, he was much in the store and therefore did not see Max when he came to call for Miriam.

From his wife he learned there had been nothing especially revealing about their meeting. Max had rung the bell and Miriam had got her coat and left with him—nothing more. Feld did not probe, for his wife was not particularly observant. Instead, he waited up for Miriam with a newspaper on his lap, which he scarcely looked at so lost was he in thinking of the future. He awoke to find her in the room with him, tiredly removing her hat. Greeting her, he was suddenly inexplicably afraid to ask anything about the evening. But since she volunteered nothing he was at last forced to inquire how she had enjoyed herself. Miriam began something non-committal but apparently changed her mind, for she said after a minute, 'I was bored.'

When Feld had sufficiently recovered from his anguished disappointment to ask why, she answered without hesitation, 'Because he's nothing more than a materialist.'

'What means this word?'

'He has no soul. He's only interested in things.'

He considered her statement for a long time but then asked, 'Will you see him again?'

'He didn't ask.'

'Suppose he will ask you?'

'I won't see him.'

He did not argue; however, as the days went by he hoped increasingly she would change her mind. He wished the boy would telephone, because he was sure there was more to him than Miriam, with her inexperienced eye, could discern. But Max didn't call. As a matter of fact he took a different route to school, no longer passing the shoemaker's store, and Feld was deeply hurt.

Then one afternoon Max came in and asked for his shoes.

The shoemaker took them down from the shelf where he had placed them, apart from the other pairs. He had done the work himself and the soles and heels were well built and firm. The shoes had been highly polished and somehow looked better than new. Max's Adam's apple went up once when he saw them, and his eyes had little lights in them.

'How much?' he asked, without directly looking at the shoemaker.

'Like I told you before,' Feld answered sadly. 'One dollar fifty cents.'

Max handed him two crumpled bills and received in return a newly minted silver half dollar.

He left. Miriam had not been mentioned. That night the shoemaker discovered that his new assistant had been all the while stealing from him, and he suffered a heart attack.

*

Though the attack was very mild, he lay in bed for three weeks. Miriam spoke of going for Sobel, but sick as he was Feld rose in wrath against the idea. Yet in his heart he knew there was no other way, and the first weary day back in the shop thoroughly convinced him, so that night after supper he dragged himself to Sobel's rooming house.

He toiled up the stairs, though he knew it was bad for him, and at the top knocked at the door. Sobel opened it and the shoemaker entered. The room was a small, poor one, with a single window facing the street. It contained a narrow cot, a low table and several stacks of books piled haphazardly around on the floor along the wall, which made him think how queer Sobel was, to be uneducated and read so much. He had once asked him, Sobel, why you read so much? and the assistant could not answer him. Did you ever study in a college some place? he had asked, but Sobel shook his head. He read, he said, to know. But to know what, the shoemaker demanded, and to know, why? Sobel never explained, which proved he read much because he was queer.

Feld sat down to recover his breath. The assistant was resting on his bed with his heavy back to the wall. His shirt and trousers were clean, and his stubby fingers, away from the shoemaker's bench, were strangely pallid. His face was thin and pale, as if he had been shut in his room since the day he had bolted from the store.

'So when you will come back to work?' Feld asked him.

To his surprise, Sobel burst out, 'Never.

Jumping up, he strode over to the window that looked out upon the miserable street. 'Why should I come back?' he cried.

'I will raise your wages.'

'Who cares for your wages?'

The shoemaker, knowing he didn't care, was at a loss what else to say.

'What do you want from me, Sobel?'

'Nothing.'

'I always treated you like you was my son.'

Sobel vehemently denied it. 'So why you look for strange boys in the street they should go out with Miriam? Why you don't think of me?'

The shoemaker's hands and feet turned freezing cold. His voice became so hoarse he couldn't speak. At last he cleared his throat and croaked, 'So what has my daughter got to do with a shoemaker thirty-five years old who works for me?'

'Why do you think I worked so long for you?' Sobel cried out. 'For the stingy wages I sacrificed five years of my life so you could have to eat and drink and where to sleep?'

'Then for what?' shouted the shoemaker.

'For Miriam,' he blurted—'for her.'

The shoemaker, after a time, managed to say, 'I pay wages in cash, Sobel,' and lapsed into silence. Though he was seething with excitement, his mind was coldly clear, and he had to admit to himself he had sensed all along that Sobel felt this way. He had never so much as thought it consciously, but he had felt it and was afraid.

'Miriam knows?' he muttered hoarsely.

'She knows.'

'You told her?'

'No.'

'Then how does she know?'

'How does she know?' Sobel said, 'because she knows. She knows who I am and what is in my heart.'

Feld had a sudden insight. In some devious way, with his books and commentary, Sobel had given Miriam to understand that he loved her. The shoemaker felt a terrible anger at him for his deceit.

'Sobel, you are crazy,' he said bitterly. 'She will never marry a man so old and ugly like you.'

Sobel turned black with rage. He cursed the shoemaker, but then, though he trembled to hold it in, his eyes filled with tears and he broke into deep sobs. With his back to Feld, he stood at the window, fists clenched, and his shoulders shook with his choked sobbing.

Watching him, the shoemaker's anger diminished. His teeth were on edge with pity for the man, and his eyes grew moist. How strange and sad that a refugee, a grown man, bald and old with his miseries, who had by the skin of his teeth escaped Hitler's incinerators, should fall in love, when he had got to America, with a girl less than half his age. Day after day, for five years, he had sat at his bench, cutting and hammering away, waiting for the girl to become a woman, unable to ease his heart with speech, knowing no protest but desperation.

'Ugly I didn't mean,' he said half aloud.

Then he realized that what he had called ugly was not Sobel but Miriam's life if she married him. He felt for his daughter a strange and gripping sorrow, as if she were already Sobel's bride, the wife, after all, of a shoemaker, and had in her life no more than her mother had had. And all his dreams for her—why he had slaved and destroyed his heart with anxiety and labour—all these dreams of a better life were dead.

The room was quiet. Sobel was standing by the window reading, and it was curious that when he read he looked young.

'She is only nineteen,' Feld said brokenly. 'This is too young yet to get married. Don't ask her for two years more, till she is twenty-one, then you can talk to her.'

Sobel didn't answer. Feld rose and left. He went slowly down the stairs but once outside, though it was an icy night and the crisp falling snow whitened the street, he walked with a stronger stride.

But the next morning, when the shoemaker arrived, heavy-hearted, to open the store, he saw he needn't have come, for his assistant was already seated at the last, pounding leather for his love.

H. E. BATES

Shot Actress—Full Story

——————

THERE were fifteen thousand people in Claypole, but only one actress. She kept a milliner's shop.

My name is Sprake. I kept the watchmaker-and-jeweller's shop next door to Miss Porteus for fifteen years. During all that time she never spoke to me. I am not sure that she ever spoke to anyone; I never saw her. My wife and I were a decent, respectable, devoted couple, Wesleyans, not above speaking to anyone, and I have been on the local stage myself, singing in oratorio, but we were never good enough for Miss Porteus. But that was her affair. If she hadn't been so standoffish she might, perhaps, have been alive today. As it is, she is dead, and she died, as everybody knows, on the front page of the newspapers.

No one in Claypole knew much about Miss Porteus. We knew she had been an actress, but where she had been an actress, and in what plays and in what theatres, and when, nobody knew. She looked like an actress: she was tall and very haughty and her hair, once blonde, was something of the colour of tobacco-stained moustaches, a queer yellowish ginger, as though the dye had gone wrong. Her lips were red and bitter; and with her haughty face she looked like a cold nasty woman in a play. She dressed, just for show, exactly the opposite of every other woman in Claypole: in winter she came out in chiffon and in summer you would see her walking across the golf-course, not speaking to anyone, in great fox furs something the colour of her own hair.

Her shop was just the same: at a time when every milliner-draper in Claypole used to cram as much into the shop window as possible, Miss Porteus introduced that style of one hat on a stand and a vase of expensive flowers on a length of velvet. But somehow that never quite came off. The solitary hat looked rather like Miss Porteus herself: lonely and haughty and out of place.

The backways of her shop and ours faced on to each other; the gardens were divided by a partition of boards and fencing, but we could see from our bathroom into Miss Porteus's bathroom. You could see a great array of fancy cosmetic bottles outlined behind the frosted glass. You could see Miss Porteus at her toilet. But you never saw anyone else there.

Then one day we did see someone else there. One Wednesday morning my wife came scuffling into the shop and behind the counter, where I was mending a tuppenny-ha'penny Swiss lever that I'd had lying about for months, and said that she'd seen a man in Miss Porteus's backyard.

'Well, what about it?' I said. 'I don't care if there's fifty men. Perhaps that's what she wants, a man or two,' I said. Just like that. I was busy and I thought no more about it. But, as it turned out afterwards, my wife did. I daresay she was a bit inquisitive, but while she was arranging the bedroom curtains she saw the man several times. She got a clear view of him: he was middle-aged and he had side-linings and he wore a yellow tie.

That night, when I went to bed, the light was burning

in Miss Porteus's bathroom, but I couldn't see Miss Porteus. Then when I went into the bathroom next morning the light was still burning. I said, 'Hullo, Miss Porteus left the light on all night,' but I thought no more about it. Then when I went up at mid-day the light was still on. It was still on that afternoon and it was on all that night.

My wife was scared. But I said, 'Oh, it's Thursday and she's taken a day off and gone up to London.' But the light went on burning all the next day and it was still burning late that night.

By that time I was puzzled myself. I went and tried Miss Porteus's shop door. It was locked. But there was really nothing strange about that. It was eleven o'clock at night and it ought to have been locked.

We went to bed, but my wife couldn't sleep. She kept saying I ought to do something. 'What can I do?' I said. At last she jumped up in bed.

'You've got to get a ladder out and climb up and see if everything's all right in Miss Porteus's bathroom,' she said.

'Oh, all right,' I said.

So I heaved our ladder over the boards and then ran it up to Miss Porteus's bathroom window. I climbed up. That was the picture they took of me later on: up the ladder, pointing to the bathroom window, which was marked with a cross. All the papers had it in.

What I saw through the bathroom window, even through the frosted glass, was bad enough, but it was only when I had telephoned to the police station and we had forced an entrance that I saw how really terrible it was.

Miss Porteus was lying on the bathroom floor with a bullet wound in her chest. We banged the door against her head as we went in. She had been dead for some time and I could almost calculate how long, because of the light. She was in a cerise pink nightgown and the blood had made a little rosette on her chest.

'Bolt the garden gate and say nothing to nobody,' the sergeant said.

I said nothing. The next morning all Claypole knew that Miss Porteus had been murdered, and by afternoon the whole of England knew. The reporter from the *Argus*, the local paper, came rushing round to see me before seven o'clock. 'Give me it,' he said. 'Give me it before they get here. I'm on linage for the *Express* and I'll rush it through. Just the bare facts. What you saw. I'll write it.' So I made a statement. It was just a plain statement, and every word of it was true.

Then just before dinner I saw three men with cameras on the opposite side of the street. They took pictures of Miss Porteus's shop, and then they came across the road into my shop. They as good as forced their way through the shop, into the backyard, and there they photographed Miss Porteus's bathroom window. Then one of the cameramen put a pound note into my hand and said, 'On top of the ladder?' The ladder was still there and I climbed up and they photographed me on top of it, pointing at the window.

By afternoon the crowd was packed thick right across the street. They were pressed tight against my window. I put the shutters up. Just as I was finishing them, four men came up and said they were newspapermen and could I give them the facts about Miss Porteus.

Before I could speak they pushed into the shop. They shut the door. Then I saw that there were not four of them but twelve. I got behind the counter and they took out notebooks and rested them on my glass showcases and scribbled. I tried to tell them what I had told the local man, the truth, and nothing more or less than the truth, but they didn't want that. They hammered me with questions.

What was Miss Porteus like? Was her real name Porteus? What else besides Porteus? What colour was her hair? How long had she been there? Did it strike me as funny that an actress should run a milliner's shop? When had I last seen the lady? About the bathroom . . . about her hair . . .

I was flustered and I said something about her hair being a little reddish, and one of the newspapermen said:

'Now we're getting somewhere. Carrots,' and they all laughed.

Then another said: 'Everybody says this woman was an actress. But where did she act? London? What theatre? When?'

'I don't know,' I said.

'You've lived next door all this time and don't know? Did you never hear anybody say if she'd been in any particular play?'

'No. I . . . Well, she was a bit strange.'

'Strange?' They seized on that. 'How? What? Mysterious?'

'Well,' I said, 'she was the sort of woman who'd come out in big heavy fox furs on a hot summer day. She was different.'

'Crazy?'

'Oh, no!'

'Eccentric?'

'No. I wouldn't say that.'

'About her acting,' they said. 'You must have heard something.'

'No.' Then I remembered something. At a rehearsal of the Choral Society, once, her name had come up and

somebody had said something about her having been in
Othello. I remember it because there was some argument
about whether Othello was a pure black or just a half-caste.

'*Othello?*' The newspapermen wrote fast. 'What was she?
Desdemona?'

'Well,' I said, 'I don't think you ought to put that in. I
don't know if it's strictly true or not. I can't vouch for it.
I don't think——'

'And this man that was seen,' they said. 'When was it?
When did you see him? What was he like?'

I said I didn't know, that I hadn't seen him, but that my
wife had. So they had my wife in. They questioned her.
They were nice to her. But they put down, as in my case, things
she did not say. Yellow tie? Dark? How dark? Foreign-
looking? Actor? Every now and then one of them dashed out
to the post office. They questioned us all that afternoon.

The next morning the placards of the morning newspapers
were all over Claypole. 'Shot Actress—Full Story.' It was
my story, but somehow, as it appeared in the papers, it was
not true. I read all the papers. They had my picture, the
picture of Miss Porteus's shop, looking somehow strange
and forlorn with its drawn blind, and a picture of Miss
Porteus herself, as she must have looked about 1920. All
over these papers were black stabbing headlines: 'Search for
Shot Actress Assailant Goes On.' 'Police anxious to Inter-
view Foreigner with Yellow Tie.' 'Real Life Desdemona:
Jealousy Victim?' 'Eccentric Actress Recluse Dead in Bathroom.' 'Mystery Life of Actress who wore Furs in Heat
Wave.' 'Beautiful Red-haired Actress who Spoke to
Nobody.' 'Disappearance of Dark-looking Foreigner.'

It was Saturday. That afternoon Claypole was besieged

by hundreds of people who had never been there before. They moved past Miss Porteus's shop and mine in a great stream, in cars and on foot and pushing bicycles, staring up at the dead actress's windows. They climbed in over the fence of my back garden and trampled on the flower-beds, until the police stopped them. Towards evening the crowd was so thick outside, in the front, that I put the shutters up again, and by six o'clock I closed the shop. The police kept moving the crowd on, but it was no use. It swarmed out of the High Street into the side street and then round by the back streets until it came into High Street again. Hundreds of people who had seen Miss Porteus's shop every day of their lives suddenly wanted to stare at it. They came to stare at the sun-faded blinds, just like any other shop blinds, as though they were jewelled; they fought to get a glimpse of the frosted pane of Miss Porteus's bathroom. All the tea shops in Claypole that day were crowded out.

We had reporters and photographers and detectives tramping about the house and the garden all that day and the next. That Sunday morning I missed going to chapel, where I used to sing tenor in the choir, for the first time for almost ten years. My wife could not sleep and she was nervously exhausted and kept crying. The Sunday newspapers were full of it again: the pictures of poor Miss Porteus, the shop, the bathroom window, my shop, the headlines. That afternoon the crowds began again, thicker than ever, and all the tea shops which normally did not open on Sunday opened and were packed out. A man started to sell souvenir photographs of Claypole High Street in the streets at threepence each, and it was as though he were selling pound notes or bits of Miss Porteus's hair. The sweet shops opened and you saw people buying Claypole rock and Claypole treacle toffee, which is a speciality of the town. The police drafted in extra men and right up to ten o'clock strange people kept going by, whole families, with children, in their Sunday clothes, staring up at Miss Porteus's windows with mouths open.

That afternoon I went for a walk, just for a few minutes, to get some air. Everybody I knew stopped me and wanted to talk, and one man I knew only slightly stopped me and said: 'What she look like, in the nightgown? See anything?' Another said: 'Ah, you don't tell me she lived there all alone for nothing. I know one man who knew his way upstairs. And where there's one you may depend there's others. She knew her way about.'

The inquest was held on the Monday. It lasted three days. My wife and I were witnesses and it came out, then, that Miss Porteus's name was not Porteus at all but Helen Williams. Porteus had been her stage name. It came out also that there was a conflict of opinion in the medical evidence, that it was not clear if Miss Porteus had been murdered or if she had taken her life. It was a very curious, baffling case, made more complicated because the man with the yellow tie had not been found, and the jury returned an open verdict.

All this made it much worse. The fact of Miss Porteus having had two names gave her an air of mystery, of duplicity, and the doubts about her death increased it. There sprang up, gradually, a different story about Miss Porteus. It began to go all over Claypole that she was a woman of a certain reputation, that the milliner's shop was a blind. 'Did you ever see anybody in there, or going in? No, nor did anybody else. Did anybody ever buy a hat there? No. But the back door was always undone.' That rumour gave cause for others. 'Sprake,' people began to say, 'told me himself that she lay on the floor naked. They put the nightgown on afterwards.' Then she became not only a woman of light virtue and naked, but also pregnant. 'That's why,' people began to say, 'she either shot herself or was shot. Take it which way you like. But I had it straight from Sprake.'

As the story of Miss Porteus grew, the story of my own part in it grew. Business had been very bad and for three days, because of the inquest, I had had to close the shop, but suddenly people began to come in. They looked out old watches and clocks that needed repairing, brooches that had been out of fashion for years and needed remodelling, and they brought them in; they came in to buy watches, knick-knacks, ashtrays, bits of jewellery, clocks, anything. A man asked for an ashtray with Claypole church on it as a souvenir.

By the week-end I was selling all the souvenirs I could lay hands on. The shop was never empty. I took my meals standing up and by the end of the day my wife and I were worn out by that extraordinary mad rush of business. We rested in bed all day on Sunday, exhausted. Then on Monday it all began again, not quite so bad, but almost. We were besieged by people coming in, ostensibly to buy something, but in reality on the chance of hearing me say something about Miss Porteus's death. I was in a dilemma: I wanted to close the shop and end it all, but somehow it wasn't possible. Business is business and death is death and you've got to live. And so I kept open.

Then the police came to see me again. The man with the yellow tie had not been found and they wanted my wife and me to go to the station to check the statements we had given. We shut the shop and drove to the station in a taxi.

We were there three hours. When we got back there was a crowd of fifty people round the shop, murmuring and pushing and arguing among themselves. The rumour had gone round that the police had arrested me.

Once that rumour had begun, nothing could stop its consequences. It was a rumour that never quite became tangible. It drifted about like smoke. It was there, but you could never grasp it. No one would really say anything, but the rumour was all over Claypole that I knew more than I would say. With one rumour went others: it began to be said that my wife and I were busybodies, Nosy Parkers. How else had we come to be squinting into Miss Porteus's bathroom? How else had we seen the man with the yellow tie in the backyard? We were Peeping Toms. I never heard anyone say this. But it was there. I saw it in people's faces: I felt it. I felt it as plainly as a man feels the change of weather in an old wound.

But there was one thing I did hear them say. I used to belong, in Claypole, to a Temperance club, the Melrose; we had four full-sized billiard tables and in the evenings I went there to play billiards and cards, to have a smoke and a talk and so on. Next to the billiard room was a small cloakroom, and one evening, as I was hanging up my coat, I heard someone at the billiard table say:

'Old Sprake knows a thing or two. Think I should be here if I had as many quid as times old Sprake's been upstairs next door? Actress, my eye. Some act. Pound a time. Ever struck you it was funny old Sprake knew the colour of that nightgown so well?'

I put on my coat again and went out of the club. I was trembling and horrified and sick. What I had heard seemed

to be the crystallization of all the rumours that perhaps were
and perhaps were not going round Claypole. It may have
been simply the crystallization of my own fears. I don't
know, I only know that I felt that I was suspected of things
I had not done and had not said; that not only was Miss
Porteus a loose woman but that I had had illicit relations
with her; that not only was she pregnant but that I, perhaps,
had had something to do with that pregnancy; that not
only had she been murdered but that I knew more than I
would say about that murder. I was harassed by fears and
counter-fears. I did not know what to do.

And all the time that mad rush of customers went on. All
day people would be coming in to buy things they did not
want, just on the off-chance of hearing me say something
about Miss Porteus's death, or of asking me some questions
about her life. It was so tiring and irritating that I had to
defend myself from it. So I hit upon the idea of saying the
same thing to everybody.

'I just don't know,' I would say. I said it to everyone.
Just that: 'I just don't know.'

I suppose I must have said those words hundreds of times a
day. I suppose I often said them whether they were necessary
or not. And when a man goes on repeating one sentence hundreds of times a day, for two or three weeks, it is only natural,
perhaps, that people should begin to wonder about his sanity.

So it crept round Claypole that I was a little queer. One
day I had to go to London on business and a man in the same
compartment as myself said to another: 'Take any murder
you like. It's always the work of somebody half sharp, a
maniac. Take that Claypole murder. Clear as daylight. The
work of somebody loopy.'

That was not directed against me, but it stirred up my fears into a great ugly, lumpy mass of doubt and terror. I could not sleep. And when I looked into the glass, after a restless night, I saw a face made queer and wretched by the strain of unresolved anxieties. I felt that I could have broken down, in the middle of that rush of customers and questions and fears and rumours, and wept like a child.

Then something happened. It was important and it suddenly filled the front pages of the newspapers again with the mystery of Miss Porteus's death. The police found the man with the yellow tie. It was a sensation.

The man was a theatrical producer named Prideaux and the police found him at Brighton. The fact that his name was French and that he was found at Brighton at once established him, in the public mind, as the murderer of Miss Porteus.

But he had an explanation. He had not come forward because, quite naturally, he was afraid. Miss Porteus was an old friend, and her death, he said, had upset him terribly. It was true that he had seen Miss Porteus just before her death, because Miss Porteus had invited him to come and see her. She needed money; the millinery business was not paying its way. She feared bankruptcy and, according to Prideaux, had threatened to take her life. Prideaux promised to lend her some money and he was back in London early that evening. He proved it. The porter of his hotel could prove it. It was also proved that people had seen Miss Porteus, alive, walking out on the golf-course, as late as five o'clock that day. The hotel porter could prove that Prideaux was in London by that time.

That was the end. It was established, beyond doubt, that Miss Porteus had taken her life. And suddenly all the mystery and sensation and horror and fascination of Miss Porteus's death became nothing. The papers were not interested in her any longer and her name never appeared in the papers again.

I no longer live at Claypole. All those odd, unrealized rumours that went round were enough to drive me mad; but they were also enough to kill my wife. Like me, she could not sleep, and the shock of it all cracked her life right across, like a piece of bone. Rumour and shock and worry killed her, and she died just after the facts of Miss Porteus's death were established. A month later I gave up the business and left the town. I could not go on. The first week before her death I had three people in the shop. All that mad inquisitiveness had hardened into indifference. Nobody wanted anything any longer. Nobody ever stopped to stare up at Miss Porteus's windows.

Poor Miss Porteus. She took her life because she was hard-up, in a fit of despair. There is no more to it than that. But nobody in Claypole ever believed that and I suppose very few people ever will. In Claypole they like to think that she was murdered; they know, because the papers said so, that she was a strange and eccentric woman; they know that she acted in a play with a black man; they know, though nobody ever really said so, that she was a loose woman and that she was pregnant and that somebody shot her for that reason; they know that she let men in and up the back stairs at a pound a time and they like to think that I was one of those men; they know that I found her naked in the bathroom and that I was a bit queer and that I knew more than I would ever say.

They know, in short, all that happened to Miss Porteus. They can never know how much has happened to me.

DAN JACOBSON

The Little Pet

THEY put the rabbit hutch at the bottom of the garden, in a sheltered position between the back fence and a bank of tall lupins that grew across the bottom of the lawn. The weather was warm and summery, and it had been like that for weeks, with only an occasional thundercloud passing overhead at night and letting fall a little rain, so that their enclosed little back garden was heavy every morning with the smell of growth and bright with the glittering of water on grass. And into the leafy, clean-smelling corner went the rabbit hutch, and the pregnant rabbit within it.

'Poor thing, she doesn't know what's happening to her.'

Martha kneeled on the ground to have a closer look at the rabbit, and her husband leaned over her, propping himself on a corner of the hutch with one hand. His movements were all quick and angular, and he made too many of them; the eye of an onlooker might have been tempted to skip the lightly dressed, light-coloured husband, and rest on the wife. She could comfortably have taken the scrutiny, for she was small and dark and pretty enough, with her broad brow and wide brown eyes. But she too—like her husband—had the strained and guilty air of the perpetually well intentioned. It was their laugh that betrayed them: only two people who had lived together for some years and were very keen on meeting each other at all points could have laughed so much like each other. It was a practised, accommodating, nervous laugh that they both had, a laugh that never lasted long but was always quick to come again, with a rattle in their throats and a chatter between their teeth. It was a pity that little Francis, their only son, who was standing silently by, did not join in their laughter too.

'She'll soon get used to being here,' Martha said to the boy, 'and then you'll be able to play with her.'

'Yes,' the little boy said.

'You'll love playing with her,' Martha said.

'Yes,' the little boy said.

'Oh, see what she's doing now,' Francis senior said. He and Martha were standing arm-in-arm, so he could easily wheel her round to see. The boy stepped forward carefully to see too, and his parents, together, made way for him, grateful for the interest he was showing. The rabbit had been bought for him, after all, and they let him stand in front of them and look. They could see easily enough, over his head.

The rabbit had been bought for little Francis, and how the parents worked in the next few weeks at the fun that the rabbit was going to provide him. How assiduously they cleaned out the hutch every day and saw to it that there was fresh water for the rabbit to drink and fresh grass for the rabbit to lie on. When it rained they brought the hutch into the kitchen and kept it there, though it was quite a job for Francis to bring the clumsy contraption of wood and wire netting through the door without scratching the paint on the doorposts, and Martha found it very much in the way when she was cooking. They fed the rabbit lettuce and carrots

and cabbage leaves, even though carrots, particularly, were
dishearteningly expensive that season. And they watched the
rabbit, talked to the rabbit, put their fingers through the
wire and waved them at the rabbit, tried to get the rabbit
to answer their calls, invented names for the rabbit, dis-
carded these names and invented better ones. They said
the rabbit looked like a grandmother, so they called it
Granny; they said the rabbit looked like the villain in a
Western, so they called it Pardner; sometimes it simply
looked sweet, they said, like a bunny that had something to
do with an Easter egg or a cold little bunny on a Christmas
card, and then they admitted, laughing rapidly and leaning
against each other, that they didn't know what they should
call it except a darling of a bunny brer rabbit. And to this
joy they added the joy of thinking of names for the little
ones the rabbit was at any time due to have. Irresponsibly
they prophesied that the rabbit would have at least seven
little bunnies, at least ten little bunnies, twenty.

'What'll we do if it has twenty?' Francis asked, mockingly
aghast.

'We'll declare it a public holiday,' Martha replied. And
then to the little boy: 'Wouldn't you like twenty little
bunnies to play with? *Twenty*. What a lot of bunnies!'

'Do rabbits ever have twenty babies?' the boy asked.

The parents looked at one another, and their laugh went
no lower than their throats. 'I don't think we know.'

'Then why did you say it will?'

'We didn't say it will, darling. We were just hoping.
Wouldn't you like twenty little bunnies to play with?'

Little Francis considered carefully for a moment before
he flatly replied, 'Yes.' His watchfulness upset his parents;

they had hoped that more of it would have been directed upon the rabbit and less of it upon themselves.

But they persisted. They persisted with the rabbit even though the rabbit was no more responsive to their humour than their son. The rabbit never really looked like a grandmother or a villain in a Western or a bunny on a Christmas card, and it never responded to their names and their games: the rabbit ate the food they gave it and went about its rabbity business in the little space it had. Loudly and laughingly, Martha and Francis insisted on how very amusing it was to have a rabbit in their back garden, how cleverly the rabbit's ears moved, how handsomely its fur lay, how intelligent its eyes were—but neither of them was keen on actually handling the rabbit, for fear of fleas, and even for fear of being bitten, for the rabbit had the look of a rabbit that would bite if it felt like it.

And, really, Martha and Francis could not help thinking sometimes, a rabbit was a strange-looking animal. Its face was so strange, with that squared, prominent shape of the central bone, cut sharply downwards, almost hammer-like, like one of those sledge-hammers that men use to break rocks. And then, a long way below the eyes, below the crown of that hammer-like bone, there was the rest of the face: the flat, almost indistinguishable nose, with the rifts of the nostrils concealed unless they were active; and below that secretive nose the mouth, with its upper lip that split so horribly in two when the animal ate, revealing shamelessly pink flesh, gaping like some kind of wound. While above all, mysteriously independent of the rest, the tall ears swung forward or lay back flat or half turned, pivoting in some crafty hollow in the skull. The rabbit was black in colour, but not entirely, for many of the hairs were tipped at the end with a strange rusty colour, a kind of red, the colour of dried blood. These tips glowed, when they caught the sunlight, so that the crouching animal looked like a drop that would be scorching to hold in the hand—a little ball of fire for which Martha and Francis had too lightly assumed responsibility. But when the sun was gone from it the rabbit in its hutch looked no more than nondescript, rusty. Only its eyes were bright and mobile then, though sometimes the whiskers and half-secret nostrils would tremble with apprehensions that Martha's or Francis's grosser faculties could not respond to in their green garden behind the fence of palings.

*

The catastrophes with the rabbit came quickly upon one another, the second within a day of the first. When the rabbit finally gave birth Francis came down one morning and found one tiny mouse-like creature crawling blindly round its mother. It had grey fur, still darkly matted, and it seemed quite blind, and the mother rabbit showed no interest in it. Confidently the adults prophesied to one another that during the day it would give birth to more, to more than one; but in the evening when Francis came back from work it was to find that no more little rabbits had been produced. 'She's hiding the little one,' Martha said. 'She hasn't moved.'

'How is the little one?'

'I don't know,' Martha said. 'I've only seen it once, and it looked so feeble. Do you know what a little rabbit is supposed to look like?' she asked her husband. 'This one looks so awful, like a kind of worm. Are they supposed to be blind? Like kittens—kittens are born blind, aren't they?'

Francis laughed, but his wife did not join him. 'And little Francis?' he asked.

'He's in the garden. He's playing. I haven't seen him watching her much.'

'And he wouldn't have seen much if he had been watching her?'

'No.'

'One little rabbit. I hope Francis doesn't remember what we promised him.'

'I hope the little rabbit is all right.'

'Oh, it is,' Francis assured his wife.

When Francis went out before supper the little rabbit was hidden under its mother. Francis junior was playing quietly in the garden; he was as quiet as ever, and as neat, with the comb-marks in his hair still showing from where his mother had combed it after lunch. He too told his father that he hadn't seen the little rabbit since the morning.

The next morning, when Francis came down early to make the coffee and put on the toast, there was still no sign of the little rabbit. But Martha's first question on waking had been about the little one, and disturbed as he was by his wife's anxiety, Francis was determined now to see it—to see if it were really the grey, blind bundle of feeble move-ment that he remembered it to be. He tempted the mother rabbit forward with some wet grass that he plucked at his feet, but she did not move; he went back into the kitchen and brought some lettuce leaves out of the larder and offered them to her, but still she did not move. He snapped his fingers, he called her—not by any of the names they had given her, but simply saying, 'Come here, come here,' but she did not come forward. So in a petulant little anger he pulled out a cane from one of the flower-beds and prodded her with it. The cane slid for a moment on the rabbit's close-packed fur and the loose skin beneath before it found a hold on the haunch. Francis jabbed, he stuck upwards, and the rabbit slowly came forward. Francis stared, with the stick in his hand. There was nothing under the rabbit.

He stared, and for a moment he turned and looked up at the window of the bedroom where Francis junior slept. Had the boy taken the little rabbit out? Had Martha? But that was madness, and his heels slipped on the wet grass as he turned and stared again at the point of his stick where the little rabbit should have been. There was nothing there.

Then Francis saw that there was something there. There were a few hairs and a few droppings, but Francis gingerly moved the stick past these, and carefully turned over a small ball of hair, and saw the dark clots of blood within it, and in the next that he turned over, and the last. They were all that was left of the little rabbit.

Francis dropped his stick. 'Martha!' he shouted. 'Martha!' He met her in the kitchen, and together they rushed to inspect what Francis had told her of. But they had time to stare only for a moment into the hutch before Francis junior appeared through the kitchen door. 'He mustn't see it,' Martha said. 'He mustn't know. Take him away, Francis, quickly!'

'Breakfast,' Francis cheerfully called, and picked up the little boy and carried him back indoors, with Martha following them both. While she was giving little Francis his breakfast the father went outside and cleared up the mess. He did not speak to the mother-rabbit, nor did he look at her. Only once, when she got in his way, did he give her a fierce unwarranted jab in the ribs with the garden trowel he was using for the job.

After breakfast the little boy was sent into the garden, and then Martha, who had been very calm and stiff during breakfast, fell upon her husband. 'I will not have that animal in my house for another single day. I can't bear it. I don't want it. You must take it to the pet shop at once.'

'But, darling, I'll be late for work.'

'I don't care if you'll be late for work. You must take it away. I will not have it here.' Martha was small and fierce, like a little fighter, and Francis could not argue with her.

'All right, darling,' he said. I'll take it in the car.'

'Do it at once.'

'All right, darling.'

He went to the garden, and for the last time picked up the clumsy hutch. But little Francis followed him.

'Where are you taking it? Where are you taking the bunny?'

'Back to the pet shop.'

'Why?'

'He has to, darling,' Martha said. 'The bunny's sick.'

'No, it's not,' the boy said, turning to his mother. He was dressed, as always, with great neatness, in a white T-shirt and a pair of khaki shorts; he was not a boy whose features anyone remembered particularly, but Martha saw to it that his clothes were always spotless.

'It is sick, darling.'

'No, it's not.'

If Martha had not been so upset she would simply have

ordered her husband to get on with what he was doing. But now she brought her hands to her mouth and from behind her knuckles she asked, 'Francis, do you know why we're taking the bunny to the pet shop?'

'Yes,' the child replied.

Martha half dropped one hand, the other remaining at her mouth. And Francis senior could not move, though he stood with his arms spreadeagled, carrying the hutch. Then Martha moved, grabbing the child by the wrist. 'Why?' she demanded, and shook his arm. 'Why?'

'I think it's because she killed the little bunny.'

'So you *know*!' Martha shrieked.

'Yes.'

'And you didn't say anything about it!' The parents looked with horror at their child. But he met their gaze.

When eventually he spoke he did not seem to be in any way excusing himself. Rather he seemed to want to help his parents by explaining, 'I saw the little bits.'

'Francis!' Martha exclaimed. Francis senior could say nothing. He could only put the hutch down, and sit on it, and get his arms akimbo. Underneath him the disturbed rabbit was scurrying, as if seeking for foothold.

Then Martha bent towards the child again. 'But why didn't you tell us?'

The child looked down at the hutch. 'Because I thought you'd take the bunny away if I told you.'

Francis senior spoke at last, with a jerk of his head and a jerk of his arms. 'And you're right. We aren't having it here for another day.' Then to silence the scurrying rabbit he gave a vicious little back-kick at the hutch beneath him. The scurrying increased in violence.

'There you are,' said the little boy.

He seemed acquiescent enough, but Martha straightened herself and moved to her husband, and took him by the arm. 'Wait,' she said, and at the tone of her voice Francis rose to meet her, and the husband and wife stood closely together. 'Francis,' Martha said softly, as if the word she had to speak might break in her mouth if she said it carelessly, 'do you love the bunny?'

She could not meet the clear grey stare the child gave her. He looked straight at her, and did not open his mouth to answer her question, like someone who would not admit that he knew the meaning of the word.

And Martha dropped her husband's arm and began to walk away. 'Let it stay,' she said. 'Let him have it.'

'But——'

'Let it stay,' Martha said from a few yards off, without looking back, still walking towards the kitchen.

'All right, then,' Francis senior said, giving the hutch a parting kick. 'But you'll have to feed it and give it water and everything else.' He began to walk after his wife. He left the hutch in the middle of their lawn.

'Yes,' the little boy said.

He waited until his father had gone into the house, then he went on his knees in front of the hutch. He put his finger through the wire netting. 'Come here,' he said to the rabbit. 'I'm not cross with you. I knew you didn't like your baby.'

KATHERINE MANSFIELD

Life of Ma Parker

WHEN the literary gentleman, whose flat old Ma Parker
cleaned every Tuesday, opened the door to her that morning,
he asked after her grandson. Ma Parker stood on the door-
mat inside the dark little hall, and she stretched out her hand
to help her gentleman shut the door before she replied. 'We
buried 'im yesterday, sir,' she said quietly.

'Oh, dear me! I'm sorry to hear that,' said the literary
gentleman in a shocked tone. He was in the middle of his
breakfast. He wore a very shabby dressing-gown and carried
a crumpled newspaper in one hand. But he felt awkward.
He could hardly go back to the warm sitting-room without
saying something—something more. Then because these
people set such store by funerals he said kindly, 'I hope the
funeral went off all right.'

'Beg parding, sir?' said old Ma Parker huskily.

Poor old bird! She did look dashed. 'I hope the funeral
was a—a—success,' said he. Ma Parker gave no answer.
She bent her head and hobbled off to the kitchen, clasping
the old fish bag that held her cleaning things and an apron
and a pair of felt shoes. The literary gentleman raised his
eyebrows and went back to his breakfast.

'Overcome, I suppose,' he said aloud, helping himself to the marmalade.

Ma Parker drew the two jetty spears out of her toque and hung it behind the door. She unhooked her worn jacket and hung that up too. Then she tied her apron and sat down to take off her boots. To take off her boots or to put them on was an agony to her, but it had been an agony for years. In fact, she was so accustomed to the pain that her face was drawn and screwed up ready for the twinge before she'd so much as untied the laces. That over, she sat back with a sigh and softly rubbed her knees. . . .

*

'Gran! Gran!' Her little grandson stood on her lap in his button boots. He'd just come in from playing in the street.

'Look what a state you've made your gran's skirt into— you wicked boy!'

But he put his arms round her neck and rubbed his cheek against hers.

'Gran, gi' us a penny!' he coaxed.

'Be off with you; Gran ain't got no pennies.'

'Yes, you 'ave.'

'No, I ain't.'

'Yes, you 'ave. Gi' us one!'

Already she was feeling for the old, squashed, black leather purse.

'Well, what'll you give your gran?'

He gave a shy little laugh and pressed closer. She felt his eyelid quivering against her cheek. 'I ain't got nothing,' he murmured. . . .

*

The old woman sprang up, seized the iron kettle off the gas stove, and took it over to the sink. The noise of the water drumming in the kettle deadened her pain, it seemed. She filled the pail, too, and the washing-up bowl.

It would take a whole book to describe the state of that kitchen. During the week the literary gentleman 'did for himself'. That is to say, he emptied the tea-leaves now and again into a jam-jar set aside for that purpose, and if he ran out of clean forks he wiped over one or two on the roller towel. Otherwise, as he explained to his friends, his 'system' was quite simple, and he couldn't understand why people made all this fuss about housekeeping.

'You simply dirty everything you've got, get a hag in once a week to clean up, and the thing's done.'

The result looked like a gigantic dustbin. Even the floor was littered with toast crusts, envelopes, cigarette ends. But Ma Parker bore him no grudge. She pitied the poor young gentleman for having no one to look after him. Out of the smudgy little window you could see an immense expanse of sad-looking sky, and whenever there were clouds they looked very worn, old clouds, frayed at the edges, with holes in them, or dark stains like tea.

While the water was heating, Ma Parker began sweeping the floor. 'Yes,' she thought, as the broom knocked, 'what with one thing and another I've had my share. I've had a hard life.'

Even the neighbours said that of her. Many a time, hobbling home with her fish bag she heard them, waiting at the corner, or leaning over the area railings, say among themselves, 'She's had a hard life, has Ma Parker.' And it was so true she wasn't in the least proud of it. It was just as if you

were to say she lived in the basement-back at Number 27.
A hard life! . . .

★

At sixteen she'd left Stratford and come up to London as
kitching-maid. Yes, she was born in Stratford-on-Avon.
Shakespeare, sir? No, people were always arsking her about
him. But she'd never heard his name until she saw it on the
theatres.

Nothing remained of Stratford except that 'sitting in the
fireplace of a evening you could see the stars through the
chimley', and 'Mother always 'ad 'er side of bacon 'anging
from the ceiling'. And there was something—a bush, there
was—at the front door, that smelt ever so nice. But the bush
was very vague. She'd only remembered it once or twice in
the hospital, when she'd been taken bad.

That was a dreadful place—her first place. She was never
allowed out. She never went upstairs except for prayers
morning and evening. It was a fair cellar. And the cook was
a cruel woman. She used to snatch away her letters from
home before she'd read them, and throw them in the range
because they made her dreamy . . . And the beedles! Would
you believe it?—until she came to London she'd never seen
a black beedle. Here Ma always gave a little laugh, as though
—not to have seen a black beedle! Well! It was as if to say
you'd never seen your own feet.

When that family was sold up she went as 'help' to a
doctor's house, and after two years there, on the run from
morning till night, she married her husband. He was a baker.

'A baker, Mrs Parker!' the literary gentleman would say.
For occasionally he laid aside his tomes and lent an ear, at

least, to this product called Life. 'It must be rather nice to be married to a baker!'

Mrs Parker didn't look so sure.

'Such a clean trade,' said the gentleman.

Mrs Parker didn't look convinced.

'And didn't you like handing the new loaves to the customers?'

'Well, sir,' said Mrs Parker, 'I wasn't in the shop above a great deal. We had thirteen little ones and buried seven of them. If it wasn't the 'ospital it was the infirmary, you might say!'

'You might, *indeed*, Mrs Parker!' said the gentleman, shuddering, and taking up his pen again.

Yes, seven had gone, and while the six were still small her husband was taken ill with consumption. It was flour on the lungs, the doctor told her at the time. . . . Her husband sat up in bed with his shirt pulled over his head, and the doctor's finger drew a circle on his back.

'Now, if we were to cut him open *here*, Mrs Parker,' said the doctor, 'you'd find his lungs chock-a-block with white powder. Breathe, my good fellow!' And Mrs Parker never knew for certain whether she saw or whether she fancied she saw a great fan of white dust come out of her poor dear husband's lips. . . .

But the struggle she'd had to bring up those six little children and keep herself to herself. Terrible it had been! Then, just when they were old enough to go to school her husband's sister came to stop with them to help things along, and she hadn't been there more than two months when she fell down a flight of steps and hurt her spine. And for five years Ma Parker had another baby—and such a one for crying!—to look after. Then young Maudie went wrong and took her sister Alice with her; the two boys emigrimated, and young Jim went to India with the army, and Ethel, the youngest, married a good-for-nothing little waiter who died of ulcers the year little Lennie was born. And now little Lennie—my grandson . . .

The piles of dirty cups, dirty dishes, were washed and dried. The ink-black knives were cleaned with a piece of potato and finished off with a piece of cork. The table was scrubbed, and the dresser and the sink that had sardine tails swimming in it. . . .

He'd never been a strong child—never from the first. He'd been one of those fair babies that everybody took for a girl. Silvery fair curls he had, blue eyes, and a little freckle like a diamond on one side of his nose. The trouble she and Ethel had had to rear that child! The things out of the news-papers they tried him with! Every Sunday morning Ethel would read aloud while Ma Parker did her washing.

'Dear Sir,—Just a line to let you know my little Myrtil was laid out for dead . . . After four bottils . . . gained 8 lb in 9 weeks, *and is still putting it on.*'

*

And then the egg-cup of ink would come off the dresser and the letter would be written, and Ma would buy a postal order on her way to work next morning. But it was no use. Nothing made little Lennie put it on. Taking him to the cemetery, even, never gave him a colour; a nice shake-up in the bus never improved his appetite.

But he was Gran's boy from the first. . . .

'Whose boy are you?' said old Ma Parker, straightening

up from the stove and going over to the smudgy window. And a little voice, so warm, so close, it half stifled her—it seemed to be in her breast under her heart—laughed out, and said, 'I'm Gran's boy!'

At that moment there was a sound of steps, and the literary gentleman appeared, dressed for walking.

'Oh, Mrs Parker, I'm going out.'

'Very good, sir.'

'And you'll find your half-crown in the tray of the inkstand.'

'Thank you, sir.'

'Oh, by the way, Mrs Parker,' said the literary gentleman quickly, 'you didn't throw away any cocoa last time you were here—did you?'

'No, sir.'

'*Very* strange. I could have sworn I left a teaspoonful of cocoa in the tin.' He broke off. He said softly and firmly, 'You'll always tell me when you throw things away—won't you, Mrs Parker?' And he walked off very well pleased with himself, convinced, in fact, he'd shown Mrs Parker that under his apparent carelessness he was as vigilant as a woman.

The door banged. She took her brushes and cloths into the bedroom. But when she began to make the bed, smoothing, tucking, patting, the thought of little Lennie was unbearable. Why did he have to suffer so? That's what she couldn't understand. Why should a little angel child have to arsk for his breath and fight for it? There was no sense in making a child suffer like that.

. . . From Lennie's little box of a chest there came a sound as though something was boiling. There was a great lump of something bubbling in his chest that he couldn't get rid of. When he coughed the sweat sprang out on his head; his eyes bulged, his hands waved, and the great lump bubbled as a potato knocks in a saucepan. But what was more awful than all was when he didn't cough he sat against the pillow and never spoke or answered, or even made as if he heard. Only he looked offended.

'It's not your poor old gran's doing it, my lovey,' said old Ma Parker, patting back the damp hair from his little scarlet ears. But Lennie moved his head and edged away. Dreadfully offended with her he looked—and solemn. He bent his head and looked at her sideways as though he couldn't have believed it of his gran.

But at the last . . . Ma Parker threw the counterpane over the bed. No, she simply couldn't think about it. It was too much—she'd had too much in her life to bear. She'd borne it up till now, she'd kept herself to herself, and never once had she been seen to cry. Never by a living soul. Not even her own children had seen Ma break down. She'd kept a proud face always. But now! Lennie gone—what had she? She had nothing. He was all she'd got from life, and now he was took too. Why must it all have happened to me? she wondered. 'What have I done?' said old Ma Parker. 'What have I done?'

As she said those words she suddenly let fall her brush. She found herself in the kitchen. Her misery was so terrible that she pinned on her hat, put on her jacket and walked out of the flat like a person in a dream. She did not know what she was doing. She was like a person so dazed by the horror of what has happened that he walks away—anywhere, as though by walking away he could escape. . . .

*

It was cold in the street. There was a wind like ice. People went flitting by, very fast; the men walked like scissors; the women trod like cats. And nobody knew—nobody cared. Even if she broke down, if at last, after all these years, she were to cry, she'd find herself in the lock-up as like as not.

But at the thought of crying it was as though little Lennie leapt in his gran's arms. Ah, that's what she wants to do, my dove. Gran wants to cry. If she could only cry now, cry for a long time, over everything, beginning with her first place and the cruel cook, going on to the doctor's, and then the seven little ones, death of her husband, the children's leaving her, and all the years of misery that led up to Lennie. But to have a proper cry over all these things would take a long time. All the same, the time for it had come. She must do it. She couldn't put it off any longer; she couldn't wait any more. . . . Where could she go?

'She's had a hard life, has Ma Parker.' Yes, a hard life, indeed! Her chin began to tremble; there was no time to lose. But where? Where?

She couldn't go home; Ethel was there. It would frighten Ethel out of her life. She couldn't sit on a bench anywhere; people would come arsking her questions. She couldn't possibly go back to the gentleman's flat; she had no right to cry in strangers' houses. If she sat on some steps a policeman would speak to her.

Oh, wasn't there anywhere where she could hide and keep herself to herself and stay as long as she liked, not disturbing anybody, and nobody worrying her? Wasn't there anywhere in the world where she could have her cry out—at last?

Ma Parker stood, looking up and down. The icy wind blew out her apron into a balloon. And now it began to rain. There was nowhere.

JOHN WAIN

A Message from the Pig-Man

HE WAS never called Ekky now, because he was getting to
be a real boy, nearly six, with grey flannel trousers that had
a separate belt and weren't kept up by elastic, and his name
was Eric. But this was just one of those changes brought
about naturally, by time, not a disturbing alteration; he
understood that. His mother hadn't meant that kind of
change when she had promised, 'Nothing will be changed.'
It was all going to go on as before, except that Dad wouldn't
be there, and Donald would be there instead. He knew
Donald, of course, and felt all right about his being in the
house, though it seemed, when he lay in bed and thought
about it, mad and pointless that Donald's coming should
mean that Dad had to go. Why should it mean that? The
house was quite big. He hadn't any brothers and sisters, and
if he *had* had any he wouldn't have minded sharing his
bedroom, even with a baby that wanted a lot of looking
after, so long as it left the spare room free for Dad to sleep
in. If he did that they wouldn't have a spare room, it was
true, but, then, the spare room was nearly always empty;
the last time anybody had used the spare room was *years*
ago, when he had been much smaller—last winter, in fact.
And, even then, the visitor, the lady with the funny teeth

57

who laughed as she breathed in, instead of as she breathed out like everyone else, had only stayed two or three nights. *Why* did grown-ups do everything in such a mad, silly way? They often told him not to be silly, but they were silly themselves in a useless way, not laughing or singing or anything, just being silly and sad.

It was so hard to read the signs; that was another thing. When they did give you something to go on, it was impossible to know how to take it. Dad had bought him a train, just a few weeks ago, and taught him how to fit the lines together. That ought to have meant that he would stay; what sensible person would buy a train, and fit it all up ready to run, even as a present for another person—*and then leave*? Donald had been quite good about the train, Eric had to admit that; he had bought a bridge for it and a lot of rolling-stock. At first he had got the wrong kind of rolling-stock, with wheels too close together to fit on to the rails; but instead of playing the usual grown-ups' trick of pulling a face and then not doing anything about it, he had gone back to the shop, straight away that same afternoon, and got the right kind. Perhaps that meant *he* was going to leave. But that didn't seem likely. Not the way Mum held on to him all the time, even holding him round the middle as if he needed keeping in one piece.

All the same, he was not Ekky now, he was Eric, and he was sensible and grown-up. Probably it was his own fault that everything seemed strange. He was not living up to his grey flannel trousers—and perhaps that was it; being afraid of too many things, not asking questions that would probably turn out to have quite simple answers.

The Pig-man, for instance. He had let the Pig-man worry

him far too much. None of the grown-ups acted as if the Pig-man was anything to be afraid of. He probably just *looked* funny, that was all. If, instead of avoiding him so carefully, he went outside one evening and looked at him, took a good long, unafraid look, leaving the back door open behind him so that he could dart in to safety and warmth of the house . . . no! It was better, after all, not to see the Pig-man; not till he was bigger, anyway; nearly six was quite big but it wasn't really *very* big. . . .

And yet it was one of those puzzling things. No one ever told him to be careful not to let the Pig-man get hold of him, or warned him in any way; so the Pig-man *must* be harmless, because when it came to anything that *could* hurt you, like the traffic on the main road, people were always ramming it into you that you must look both ways, and all that stuff. And yet when it came to the Pig-man no one ever mentioned him; he seemed beneath the notice of grown-ups. His mother would say, now and then, 'Let me see, it's today the Pig-man comes, isn't it?' or, 'Oh dear, the Pig-man will be coming round soon, and I haven't put anything out.' If she talked like this Eric's spine would tingle and go cold; he would keep very still and wait, because quite often her next words would be, 'Eric, just take these peelings,' or whatever it was, 'out to the bucket, dear, will you?' The bucket was about fifty yards away from the back door; it was shared by the people in the two next-door houses. None of *them* was afraid of the Pig-man, either. What was their attitude? he wondered. Were they sorry for him, having to eat damp old stuff out of a bucket—tea-leaves and eggshells and that sort of thing? Perhaps he cooked it when he got home, and made it a bit nicer. Certainly, it didn't

look too nice when you lifted the lid of the bucket and saw
it all lying there. It sometimes smelt, too. Was the Pig-man
very poor? Was he sorry for himself, or did he feel all right
about being like that? *Like what?* What did the Pig-man
look like? He would have little eyes, and a snout with a
flat end; but would he have trotters, or hands and feet
like a person's?

Lying on his back, Eric worked soberly at the problem.
The Pig-man's bucket had a handle; so he must carry it in
the ordinary way, in his hand—unless, of course, he walked
on all fours and carried it in his mouth. But that wasn't
very likely, because if he walked on all fours what difference
would there be between him and an ordinary pig? To be
called the Pig-man, rather than the Man-pig, surely implied
that he was upright, and dressed. Could he talk? Probably,
in a kind of grunting way, or else how could he tell the
people what kind of food he wanted them to put in his
bucket? *Why hadn't he asked Dad about the Pig-man?* That
had been his mistake; Dad would have told him exactly
all about it. But he had gone. Eric fell asleep, and in his sleep
he saw Dad and the Pig-man going in a train together; he
called, but they did not hear and the train carried them away.
'Dad!' he shouted desperately after it. 'Don't bring the
Pig-man when you come back! Don't bring the Pig-man!'
Then his mother was in the room, kissing him and smelling
nice; she felt soft, and the softness ducked him into sleep,
this time without dreams; but the next day his questions
returned.

Still, there was school in the morning, and going down to
the swings in the afternoon, and altogether a lot of different
things to crowd out the figure of the Pig-man and the

questions connected with him. And Eric was never farther from worrying about it all than that moment, a few evenings later, when it suddenly came to a crisis.

Eric had been allowed, 'just for once', to bring his train into the dining-room after tea, because there was a fire there that made it nicer than the room where he usually played. It was warm and bright, and the carpet in front of the fireplace was smooth and firm, exactly right for laying out the rails on. Donald had come home and was sitting—in Dad's chair, but never mind—reading the paper and smoking. Mum was in the kitchen, clattering gently about, and both doors were open so that she and Donald could call out remarks to each other. Only a short passage lay between. It was just the part of the day Eric liked best, and bed-time was comfortably far off. He fitted the sections of rail together, glancing in anticipation at the engine as it stood proudly waiting to haul the carriages round and round, tremendously fast.

Then his mother called: 'Eric! Do be a sweet, good boy, and take this stuff out for the Pig-man. My hands are covered with cake mixture. I'll let you scrape out the basin when you come in.'

For a moment he kept quite still, hoping he hadn't really heard her say it, that it was just a voice inside his head. But Donald looked over at him and said: 'Go along, old man. You don't mind, do you?'

Eric said, 'But tonight's when the Pig-man *comes*.'

Surely, *surely* they weren't asking him to go out, in the deep twilight, just at the time when there was the greatest danger of actually *meeting* the Pig-man?

'All the better,' said Donald, turning back to his paper.

Why was it better? Did they *want* him to meet the Pig-man?

Slowly, wondering why his feet and legs didn't refuse to move, Eric went through into the kitchen. 'There it is,' his mother said, pointing to a brown-paper carrier full of potato-peelings and scraps.

He took it up and opened the back door. If he was quick, and darted along to the bucket *at once*, he would be able to lift the lid, throw the stuff in quickly, and be back in the house in about the time it took to count ten.

One—two—three—four—five—six. He stopped. The bucket wasn't there.

It had gone. Eric peered round, but the light, though faint, was not as faint as *that*. He could see that the bucket had gone. *The Pig-man had already been.*

Seven—eight—nine—ten, his steps were joyous and light. Back in the house, where it was warm and bright and his train was waiting.

'The Pig-man's gone, Mum. The bucket's not there.'

She frowned, hands deep in the pudding-basin. 'Oh, yes, I do believe I heard him. But it was only a moment ago. Yes, it was just before I called you, darling. It must have been that that made me think of it.'

'Yes?' he said politely, putting down the carrier.

'So if you nip along, dear, you can easily catch him up. And I *do* want that stuff out of the way.'

'Catch him up?' he asked, standing still in the doorway.

'Yes, dear, *catch him up*,' she answered rather sharply (the Efficient Young Mother knows when to be Firm). 'He can't possibly be more than a very short way down the road.'

Before she had finished Eric was outside the door and

running. This was a technique he knew. It was the same as getting into icy-cold water. If it was the end, if the Pig-man seized him by the hand and dragged him off to his hut, well, so much the worse. Swinging the paper carrier in his hand, he ran fast through the dusk.

The back view of the Pig-man was much as he had expected it to be. A slow, rather lurching gait, hunched shoulders, an old hat crushed down on his head (to hide his ears?), and the pail in his hand. Plod, plod, as if he were tired. Perhaps this was just a ruse, though; probably he could pounce quickly enough when his wicked little eyes saw a nice tasty little boy or something . . . did the Pig-man eat birds? Or cats?

Eric stopped. He opened his mouth to call to the Pig-man, but the first time he tried nothing came out except a small rasping squeak. His heart was banging like fireworks going off. He could hardly hear anything.

'Mr Pig-man!' he called, and this time the words came out clear and rather high.

The jogging old figure stopped, turned, and looked at him. Eric could not see properly from where he stood. But he *had* to see. Everything, even his fear, sank and drowned in the raging tide of his curiosity. He moved forward. With each step he saw more clearly. The Pig-man was just an ordinary old man.

'Hello, sonny. Got some stuff there for the old grunters?'

Eric nodded, mutely, and held out his offering. What old grunters? What did he mean?

The Pig-man put down his bucket. He had ordinary hands, ordinary arms. He took the lid off. Eric held out the paper carrier, and the Pig-man's hand actually touched his own for a second. A flood of gratitude rose up inside him. The Pig-man tipped the scraps into the bucket and handed the carrier back.

'Thanks, sonny,' he said.

'Who's it for?' Eric asked, with another rush of articulateness. His voice seemed to have a life of its own.

The Pig-man straightened up, puzzled. Then he laughed, in a gurgling sort of way, but not like a pig at all.

'Arh Aarh Harh Harh,' the Pig-man went. 'Not for me, if that's whatcher mean, arh harh.'

He put the lid back on the bucket. 'It's for the old grunters,' he said. 'The old porkers. Just what they likes. Only not fruit skins. I leaves a note, sometimes, about what not to put in. Never fruit skins. It gives 'em the belly-ache.'

He was called the Pig-man because he had some pigs that he looked after.

'Thank you,' said Eric. 'Good night.' He ran back towards the house, hearing the Pig-man, the ordinary old man, the ordinary, usual, normal old man, say in his just ordinary old man's voice, 'Good night, sonny.'

So that was how you did it. You just went straight ahead, not worrying about this or that. Like getting into cold water. You just *did* it.

He slowed down as he got to the gate. For instance, if there was a question that you wanted to know the answer to, and you had always just felt you couldn't ask, the thing to do was to ask it. Just straight out, like going up to the Pig-man. Difficult things, troubles, questions, you just treated them like the Pig-man.

So that was it!

The warm light shone through the crack of the door. He

opened it and went in. His mother was standing at the table, her hands still working the cake mixture about. She would let him scrape out the basin, and the spoon—he would ask for the spoon, too. But not straight away. There was a more important thing first.

He put the paper carrier down and went up to her. 'Mum,' he said. 'Why can't Dad be with us even if Donald *is* here? I mean, why can't he live with us as well as Donald?'

His mother turned and went to the sink. She put the tap on and held her hands under it.

'Darling,' she called.

'Yes?' came Donald's voice.

'D'you know what he's just said?'

'What?'

'He's just asked . . .' She turned the tap off and dried her hands, not looking at Eric. 'He wants to know why we can't have Jack to live with us.'

There was a silence, then Donald said, quietly, so that his voice only just reached Eric's ears, 'That's a hard one.'

'You can scrape out the basin,' his mother said to Eric. She lifted him up and kissed him. Then she rubbed her cheek along his, leaving a wet smear. 'Poor little Ekky,' she said in a funny voice.

She put him down and he began to scrape out the pudding-basin, certain at least of one thing, that grown-ups were mad and silly and he hated them all, all, *all*.

IRWIN SHAW

The Dry Rock

———◇———

'WE'RE late,' Helen said, as the cab stopped at a light. 'We're twenty minutes late.' She looked at her husband accusingly.

'All right,' Fitzsimmons said. 'I couldn't help it. The work was on the desk and it had to——'

'This is the one dinner party of the year I didn't want to be late for,' Helen said. 'So naturally——'

The cab started and was halfway across the street when the Ford sedan roared into it, twisting, with a crashing and scraping of metal, a high mournful scream of brakes, the tinkling of glass. The cab shook a little, then subsided.

The cabby, a little grey man, turned and looked back worriedly. 'Everybody is all right?' he asked nervously.

'Everybody is fine,' Helen said bitterly, pulling at her cape to get it straight again after the jolting.

'No damage done,' said Fitzsimmons, smiling reassuringly at the cabby, who looked very frightened.

'I am happy to hear that,' the cabby said. He got out of his car and stood looking sadly at his fender, now thoroughly crumpled, and his headlight, now without a lens. The door of the Ford opened and its driver sprang out. He was a large young man with a light grey hat. He glanced hurriedly at the cab.

'Why don't yuh watch where the hell yer going?' he asked harshly.

'The light was in my favour,' said the cabby. He was a small man of fifty, in a cap and a ragged coat, and he spoke with a heavy accent. 'It turned green and I started across. I would like your licence, mister.'

'What for?' the man in the grey hat shouted. 'Yer load's all right. Get on yer way. No harm done.' He started back to his car.

The cabby gently put his hand on the young man's arm. 'Excuse me, friend,' he said. 'It is a five dollar job, at least. I would like to see your licence.'

The young man pulled his arm away, glared at the cabby. 'Aaah,' he said and swung. His fist made a loud, surprising noise against the cabby's nose. The old man sat down slowly on the running-board of his cab, holding his head wearily in his hands. The young man in the grey hat stood over him, bent over, fists still clenched. 'Didn't I tell yuh no harm was done?' he shouted. 'Why didn't yuh lissen t'me? I got a good mind to——'

'Now, see here,' Fitzsimmons said, opening the rear door and stepping out.

'What d'*you* want?' The young man turned and snarled at Fitzsimmons, his fists held higher. 'Who asked for *you*?'

'I saw the whole thing,' Fitzsimmons began, 'and I don't think you——'

'Aaah,' snarled the young man. 'Dry up.'

'Claude,' Helen called. 'Claude, keep out of this.'

'Claude,' the young man repeated balefully. 'Dry up, Claude.'

'Are you all right?' Fitzsimmons asked, bending over the cabby, who still sat reflectively on the running-board, his head down, his old and swollen cap hiding his face, blood trickling down his clothes.

'I'm all right,' the cabby said wearily. He stood up, looked wonderingly at the young man. 'Now, my friend, you force me to make trouble. Police!' he called, loudly. '*Police!*'

'Say, lissen,' the man in the grey hat shouted. 'What the hell do yuh need to call the cops for? Hey, cut it out!'

'*Police!*' the old cabby shouted calmly, but with fervour deep in his voice. 'Police!'

'I ought to give it to yuh good.' The young man shook his fist under the cabby's nose. He jumped around nervously. 'This is a small matter,' he shouted, 'nobody needs the cops!'

'Police!' called the cabby.

'Claude,' Helen put her head out the window. 'Let's get out of here and let the two gentlemen settle this any way they please.'

I apologize!' The young man held the cabby by his lapels with both large hands, shook him, to emphasize his apology. 'Excuse me. I'm sorry. Stop yelling police, for God's sake!

'I'm going to have you locked up,' the cabby said. He stood there, slowly drying the blood off his shabby coat with his cap. His hair was grey, but long and full, like a musician's. He had a big head for his little shoulders, and a sad, lined little face and he looked older than fifty, to Fitzsimmons, very poor, neglected, badly nourished. 'You have committed a crime,' the cabby said, 'and there is a punishment for it.'

'Will yuh talk to him?' The young man turned savagely to Fitzsimmons. 'Will yuh tell him I'm sorry?'

'It's entirely up to him,' Fitzsimmons said.

'We're a half-hour late,' Helen announced bitterly. 'The perfect dinner guests.'

'It is not enough to be sorry,' said the cab-driver. '*Police . . .*'

'Say, listen, Bud,' the young man said, his voice quick and confidential. 'What's yer name?'

'Leopold Tarloff,' the cabby said. 'I have been driving a cab on the streets of New York for twenty years, and everybody thinks just because you're a cab-driver they can do whatever they want to you.'

'Lissen, Leopold,' the young man pushed his light grey hat far back on his head. 'Let's be sensible. I hit yer cab. All right. I hit you. All right.'

'What's all right about it?' Tarloff asked.

'What I mean is, I admit it, I confess I did it, that's what I mean. All right.' The young man grabbed Tarloff's short ragged arms as he spoke, intensely. 'Why the fuss? It happens every day. Police are unnecessary. I'll tell yuh what I'll do with yuh, Leopold. Five dollars, yuh say, for the fender. All right. And for the bloody nose, another pound. What do yuh say? Everybody is satisfied. Yuh've made yerself a fiver on the transaction; these good people go to their party without no more delay.'

Tarloff shook his arms free from the huge hands of the man in the grey hat. He put his head back and ran his fingers through his thick hair and spoke coldly. 'I don't want to hear another word. I have never been so insulted in my whole life.'

The young man stepped back, his arms wide, palms up wonderingly. 'I insult him!' He turned to Fitzsimmons. 'Did you hear me insult this party?' he asked.

'Claude!' Helen called. 'Are we going to sit here all night?'

'A man steps up and hits me in the nose,' Tarloff said. 'He thinks he makes everything all right with five dollars. He is mistaken. Not with five hundred dollars.'

'How much d'yuh think a clap in the puss is worth?' the young man growled. 'Who d'yuh think y'are—Joe Louis?'

'Not ten thousand dollars,' Tarloff said, on the surface calm, but quivering underneath. 'Not for twenty thousand dollars. My dignity.'

'His dignity!' the young man whispered. 'For Christ's sake!'

'What do you want to do?' Fitzsimmons asked, conscious of Helen glooming in the rear seat of the cab.

'I would like to take him to the station house and make a complaint,' Tarloff said. 'You would have to come with me, if you'd be so kind. What is your opinion on the matter?'

'Will yuh tell him the cops are not a necessity!' the young man said hoarsely.

'Claude!' called Helen.

'It's up to you,' Fitzsimmons said, looking with what he hoped was an impartial, judicious expression at Tarloff, hoping he wouldn't have to waste any more time. 'You do what you think you ought to do.'

Tarloff smiled, showing three yellow teeth in the front of his small and childlike mouth, curved and red and surprising in the lined and weatherbeaten old hackie's face.

'Thank you very much,' he said. 'I am glad to see you agree with me.'

Fitzsimmons sighed.

*

'Yer drivin' me crazy!' the young man shouted at Tarloff. 'Yer makin' life impossible!'

'To you,' Tarloff said with dignity, 'I talk from now on only in a court of law. That's my last word.'

The young man stood there, breathing heavily, his fists clenching and unclenching, his pale grey hat shining in the light of a street lamp. A policeman turned the corner, walking in a leisurely and abstracted manner, his eyes on the legs of a girl across the street.

Fitzsimmons went over to him. 'Officer,' he said, 'there's a little job for you over here.' The policeman regretfully took his eyes off the girl's legs and sighed and walked slowly over to where the two cars were still nestling against each other.

'What are yuh?' the young man was asking Tarloff, when Fitzsimmons came up with the policeman. 'Yuh don't act like an American citizen. What are yuh?'

'I'm a Russian,' Tarloff said. 'But I'm in the country twenty-five years now, I know what the rights of an individual are.'

'Yeah,' said the young man hopelessly. 'Yeah . . .'

The Fitzsimmonses drove silently to the police station in the cab, with Tarloff driving slowly and carefully, though with hands that shook on the wheel. The policeman drove with the young man in the young man's Ford. Fitzsimmons saw the Ford stop at a cigar store and the young man jump out and go into the store, into a telephone booth.

'For three months,' Helen said, as they drove, 'I've been trying to get Adele Lowrie to invite us to dinner. Now we've finally managed it. Perhaps we ought to call her and invite the whole party down to night court.'

'It isn't night court,' Fitzsimmons said patiently. 'It's a police station. And I think you might take it a little better. After all, the poor old man has no one else to speak up for him.'

'Leopold Tarloff,' Helen said. 'It sounds impossible. Leopold Tarloff. Leopold Tarloff.'

They sat in silence until Tarloff stopped the cab in front of the police station and opened the door for them. The Ford with the policeman and the young man drove up right behind them and they all went in together.

There were some people up in front of the desk lieutenant, a dejected-looking man with long moustaches and a loud, blonde woman who kept saying that the man had threatened her with a baseball bat three times that evening. Two Negroes with bloody bandages around their heads were waiting, too.

'It will take some time,' said the policeman. 'There are two cases ahead of you. My name is Kraus.'

'Oh, my,' said Helen.

'You'd better call Adele,' Fitzsimmons said. 'Tell her not to hold dinner for us.'

Helen held out her hand gloomily for nickels.

'I'm sorry,' Tarloff said anxiously, 'to interrupt your plans for the evening.'

'Perfectly all right,' Fitzsimmons said, trying to screen

his wife's face from Tarloff by bending over to search for the nickels in his pocket.

Helen went off, disdainfully holding her long formal skirt up with her hand, as she walked down the spit- and butt-marked corridor of the police station towards a pay telephone. Fitzsimmons reflectively watched her elegant back retreat down the hallway.

'I am tired,' Tarloff said. 'I think I will have to sit down, if you will excuse me.' He sat on the floor, looking up with a frail, apologetic smile on his red face worn by wind and rain and traffic policemen. Fitzsimmons suddenly felt like crying, watching the old man sitting there among the spit and cigarette butts, on the floor against the wall, with his cap off and his great bush of musician's grey hair giving the lie to the tired, weathered face below it.

Four men threw open the outside doors and walked into the police station with certainty and authority. They all wore the same light grey hats with the huge flat brims. The young man who had hit Tarloff greeted them guardedly. 'I'm glad you're here, Pidgear,' he said to the man who by some subtle mixture of stance and clothing, of lift of eyebrow and droop of mouth, announced himself as leader.

They talked swiftly and quietly in a corner.

'A Russian!' Pidgear's voice rang out angrily. 'There are ten thousand cab-drivers in the metropolitan area, you have to pick a Russian to punch in the nose!'

'I'm excitable!' the young man yelled. 'Can I help it if I'm excitable? My father was the same way; it's a family characteristic.'

'Go tell that to the Russian,' Pidgear said. He went over

to one of the three men who had come in with him, a large
man who needed a shave and whose collar was open at the
throat, as though no collar could be bought large enough to
go all the way round that neck. The large man nodded,
went over to Tarloff, still sitting patiently against the wall.

'You speak Russian?' the man with the open collar said
to Tarloff.

'Yes, sir,' Tarloff said.

The large man sat down slowly beside him, gripped
Tarloff's knee confidentially in his tremendous hairy hand,
spoke excitedly, winningly, in Russian.

Pidgear and the young man who had hit Tarloff came over
to Fitzsimmons, leaving the other two men in the grey hats,
small, dark men with shining eyes, who just stood at the
door and looked hotly on.

'My name is Pidgear,' the man said to Fitzsimmons, who
by now was impressed with the beautiful efficiency of the
system that had been put into motion by the young driver
of the Ford—an obviously legal mind like Pidgear, a man
who spoke Russian, and two intense men with grey hats
standing on call just to see justice done, and all collected in
the space of fifteen minutes. 'Alton Pidgear,' the man said,
smiling professionally at Fitzsimmons. 'I represent Mr Rusk.'

'Yeah,' said the young man.

'My name is Fitzsimmons.'

'Frankly, Mr Fitzsimmons,' Pidgear said, 'I would like
to see you get Mr Tarloff to call this whole thing off. It's an
embarrassing affair for all concerned; nobody stands to gain
anything by pressing it.'

Helen came back and Fitzsimmons saw by the expression
on her face that she wasn't happy. 'They're at the soup by

now,' she said loudly to Fitzsimmons. 'Adele said for us to take all the time we want, they're getting along fine.'

'Mr Rusk is willing to make a handsome offer,' Pidgear said. 'Five dollars for the car, five dollars for the nose . . .'

'Go out to dinner with your husband,' Helen muttered, 'and you wind up in a telephone booth in a police station. "Excuse me for being late, darling, but I'm calling from the Eighth Precinct, this is our night for street-fighting." '

'Sssh, Helen, please,' Fitzsimmons said. He hadn't eaten since nine that morning and his stomach was growling with hunger.

'It was all a mistake,' Pidgear said smoothly. 'A natural mistake. Why should the man be stubborn? He is being reimbursed for everything, isn't he? I wish you would talk to him, Mr Fitzsimmons; we don't want to keep you from your social engagements. Undoubtedly,' Pidgear said, eyeing their evening clothes respectfully, 'you and the madam were going to an important dinner party. It would be too bad to spoil an important dinner party for a little thing like this. Why, this whole affair is niggling,' he said, waving his hand in front of Fitzsimmons's face. 'Absolutely niggling.'

Fitzsimmons looked over to where Tarloff and the other Russian were sitting on the floor. From Tarloff's face and gestures, even though he was talking in deepest Russian, Fitzsimmons could tell Tarloff was still as firm as ever. Fitzsimmons looked closely at Rusk, who was standing looking at Tarloff through narrow, baleful eyes.

'Why're you so anxious?' Fitzsimmons asked.

Rusk's eyes clouded over and his throat throbbed against his collar with rage. 'I don't want to appear in court!' he

yelled. 'I don't want the whole goddamn' business to start
all over again, investigation, lawyers, fingerprints . . .'

Pidgear punched him savagely in the ribs, his fist going a
short distance, but with great violence.

'Why don't you buy time on the National Broadcasting
System?' Pidgear asked. 'Make an address, coast to coast!'

Rusk glared murderously for a moment at Pidgear, then
leaned over towards Fitzsimmons, pointing a large blunt
finger at him. 'Do I have to put my finger in your mouth?'
he whispered hoarsely.

'What does he mean by that?' Helen asked loudly. 'Put
his finger in your mouth? Why should he put his finger in
your mouth?'

Rusk looked at her with complete hatred, turned, too full
for words, and stalked away, with Pidgear after him. The
two little men in the grey hats watched the room without
moving.

'Claude?' Helen began.

'Obviously,' Fitzsimmons said, his voice low, 'Mr Rusk
isn't anxious for anyone to look at his fingerprints. He's
happier this way.'

'You picked a fine night!' Helen shook her head sadly.
'Why can't we just pick up and get out of here?'

Rusk, with Pidgear at his side, strode back. He stopped
in front of the Fitzsimmonses. 'I'm a family man,' he said,
trying to sound like one. 'I ask yuh as a favour. Talk to
the Russian.'

'I had to go to Bergdorf Goodman,' Helen said, too deep
in her own troubles to bother with Rusk, 'to get a gown to
spend the evening in a police station. "Mrs Claude Fitzsimmons was lovely last night in blue velvet and silver fox

at Officer Kraus's reception at the Eighth Precinct. Other guests were the well-known Leopold Tarloff, and the Messrs Pidgear and Rusk, in grey hats. Other guests included the Russian Ambassador and two leading Italian artillerymen, also in grey hats." '

Pidgear laughed politely. 'Your wife is a very witty woman,' he said.

'Yes,' said Fitzsimmons, wondering why he'd married her.

'Will yuh for Christ's sake *ask*?' Rusk demanded. 'Can it hurt yuh?'

'We're willing to do our part,' Pidgear said. 'We even brought down a Russian to talk to him and clear up any little points in his own language. No effort is too great.'

Fitzsimmons's stomach growled loudly. 'Haven't eaten all day,' he said, embarrassed.

'That's what happens,' Pidgear said. 'Naturally.'

'Yeah,' said Rusk.

'Perhaps I should go out and get you a malted milk,' Helen suggested coldly.

Fitzsimmons went over to where Tarloff was sitting with the other Russian. The others followed him.

'Are you sure, Mr Tarloff,' Fitzsimmons said, 'that you still want to prosecute?'

'Yes,' Tarloff said promptly.

'Ten dollars,' Rusk said. 'I offer yuh ten dollars. Can a man do more?'

'Money is not the object.' With his cap, Tarloff patted his nose, which was still bleeding slowly and had swelled enormously, making Tarloff look lop-sided and monstrous.

'What's the object?' Rusk asked.

'The object, Mr Rusk, is principle.'

'You talk to him,' Rusk said to Fitzsimmons.

'All right,' Officer Kraus said; 'you can go up there now.'

They all filed in in front of the lieutenant sitting high at his desk.

Tarloff told his story, the accident, the wanton punch in the nose.

'It's true,' Pidgear said, 'that there was an accident, that there was a slight scuffle after by mistake. But the man isn't hurt. A little swelling in the region of the nose. No more.' He pointed dramatically to Tarloff.

'Physically,' Tarloff said, clutching his cap, talking with difficulty because his nose was clogged, 'physically that's true. I am not badly hurt. But in a mental sense . . .' He shrugged. 'I have suffered an injury.'

'Mr Rusk is offering the amount of ten dollars,' Pidgear said. 'Also, he apologizes; he's sorry.'

The lieutenant looked wearily down at Rusk. 'Are you sorry?' he asked.

'I'm sorry,' said Rusk, raising his right hand. 'On the Bible, I swear I'm sorry.'

'Mr Tarloff,' the lieutenant said, 'if you wish to press charges there are certain steps you will have to take. A deposition will have to be taken. Have you got witnesses?'

'Here,' Tarloff said with a shy smile at the Fitzsimmonses.

'They will have to be present,' the lieutenant said sleepily.

'Oh God,' Helen said.

'A warrant will have to be sworn out, there must be a hearing, at which the witnesses must also be present. . . .'

'Oh God,' Helen said.

'Then the trial,' said the lieutenant.

'Oh God,' Helen said loudly.

'The question is, Mr Tarloff,' said the lieutenant, yawning, 'are you willing to go through all that trouble?'

'The fact is,' Tarloff said unhappily, 'he hit me in the head without provocation. He is guilty of a crime on my person. He insulted me. He did me an injustice. The law exists for such things. One individual is not to be hit by another individual in the streets of the city without legal punishment.' Tarloff was using his hands to try to get everyone, the Fitzsimmonses, the lieutenant, Pidgear, to understand. 'There is a principle. The dignity of the human body. Justice. For a bad act a man suffers. It's an important thing. . . .'

'I'm excitable,' Rusk shouted. 'If yuh want, yuh can hit me in the head.'

'That is not the idea,' Tarloff said.

'The man is sorry,' the lieutenant said, wiping his eyes; 'he is offering you the sum of ten dollars; it will be a long, hard job to bring this man to trial; it will cost a lot of the taxpayers' money; you are bothering these good people here who have other things to do. What is the sense in it, Mr Tarloff?'

Tarloff scraped his feet slowly on the dirty floor, looked sadly, hopefully, at Fitzsimmons. Fitzsimmons looked at his wife, who was glaring at Tarloff, tapping her foot sharply again and again. Fitzsimmons looked back at Tarloff, standing there, before the high desk, small, in his ragged coat and wild grey hair, his little worn face twisted and grotesque with the swollen nose, his eyes lost and appealing. Fitzsimmons shrugged sadly. Tarloff drooped inside his old coat, shook his head wearily, shrugged, deserted once and for all, before the lieutenant's desk, on the dry rock of principle.

'O.K.,' he said.

'Here.' Rusk brought the ten-dollar bill out with magical speed.

Tarloff pushed it away. 'Get out of here,' he said without looking up.

No one talked all the way to Adele Lowrie's house. Tarloff opened the door and sat, looking straight ahead, while they got out. Helen went to the door of the house and rang. Silently, Fitzsimmons offered Tarloff the fare. Tarloff shook his head. 'You have been very good,' he said. 'Forget it.'

Fitzsimmons put the money away slowly.

'Claude!' Helen called. 'The door's open.'

Fitzsimmons hated his wife, suddenly, without turning to look at her. He put out his hand and Tarloff shook it wearily.

'I'm awfully sorry,' Fitzsimmons said. 'I wish I . . .'

Tarloff shrugged. 'That's all right,' he said. 'I understand.' His face, in the shabby light of the cab, worn and old and battered by the streets of the city, was a deep well of sorrow. 'There is no time. Principle.' He laughed, shrugged. 'Today there is no time for anything.'

He shifted gears and the taxi moved slowly off, its motor grinding noisily.

'Claude!' Helen called.

'Oh, shut up!' Fitzsimmons said as he turned and walked into Adele Lowrie's house.

DORIS LESSING

Through the Tunnel

———————

GOING to the shore on the first morning of the holiday, the young English boy stopped at a turning of the path and looked down at a wild and rocky bay, and then over to the crowded beach he knew so well from other years. His mother walked on in front of him, carrying a bright-striped bag in one hand. Her other arm, swinging loose, was very white in the sun. The boy watched that white, naked arm, and turned his eyes, which had a frown behind them, towards the bay and back again to his mother. When she felt he was not with her, she swung round. 'Oh, there you are, Jerry!' she said. She looked impatient, then smiled. 'Why, darling, would you rather not come with me? Would you rather . . .' She frowned, conscientiously worrying over what amusements he might secretly be longing for which she had been too busy or too careless to imagine. He was very familiar with that anxious, apologetic smile. Contrition sent him running after her. And yet, as he ran, he looked back over his shoulder at the wild bay; and all morning, as he played on the safe beach, he was thinking of it.

Next morning, when it was time for the routine of swimming and sunbathing, his mother said: 'Are you tired of the usual beach, Jerry? Would you like to go somewhere else?'

'Oh, no!' he said quickly, smiling at her out of that unfailing impulse of contrition—a sort of chivalry. Yet, walking down the path with her, he blurted out, 'I'd like to go and have a look at those rocks down there.'

She gave the idea her attention. It was a wild-looking place, and there was no one there, but she said: 'Of course, Jerry. When you've had enough, come to the big beach. Or just go straight back to the villa, if you like.' She walked away, that bare arm, now slightly reddened from yester-day's sun, swinging. And he almost ran after her again, feeling it unbearable that she should go by herself, but he did not.

She was thinking: 'Of course he's old enough to be safe without me. Have I been keeping him too close? He mustn't feel he ought to be with me. I must be careful.'

He was an only child, eleven years old. She was a widow. She was determined to be neither possessive nor lacking in devotion. She went worrying off to her beach.

As for Jerry, once he saw that his mother had gained her beach, he began the steep descent to the bay. From where he was, high up among red-brown rocks, it was a scoop of moving bluish green fringed with white. As he went lower, he saw that it spread among small promontories and inlets of rough, sharp rock, and the crisping, lapping surface showed stains of purple and darker blue. Finally, as he ran sliding and scraping down the last few yards, he saw an edge of white surf, and the shallow, luminous movement of water over white sand, and, beyond that, a solid, heavy blue.

He ran straight into the water and began swimming. He was a good swimmer. He went out fast over the gleaming sand, over a middle region where rocks lay like discoloured monsters under the surface, and then he was in the real sea— a warm sea where irregular cold currents from the deep water shocked his limbs.

When he was so far out that he could look back not only on the little bay but past the promontory that was between it and the big beach, he floated on the buoyant surface and looked for his mother. There she was, a speck of yellow under an umbrella that looked like a slice of orange peel. He swam back to shore, relieved at being sure she was there, but all at once very lonely.

On the edge of a small cape that marked the side of the bay away from the promontory was a loose scatter of rocks. Above them, some boys were stripping off their clothes. They came running, naked, down to the rocks. The English boy swam towards them, and kept his distance at a stone's throw. They were of that coast, all of them burned smooth dark brown, and speaking a language he did not understand. To be with them, of them, was a craving that filled his whole body. He swam a little closer; they turned and watched him with narrowed, alert dark eyes. Then one smiled and waved. It was enough. In a minute he had swum in and was on the rocks beside them, smiling with a desperate, nervous supplication. They shouted cheerful greetings at him, and then, as he preserved his nervous, uncomprehending smile, they understood that he was a foreigner strayed from his own beach, and they proceeded to forget him. But he was happy. He was with them.

They began diving again and again from a high point into

a well of blue sea between rough, pointed rocks. After they had dived and come up, they swam round, hauled themselves up, and waited their turn to dive again. They were big boys—men to Jerry. He dived, and they watched him, and when he swam round to take his place, they made way for him. He felt he was accepted, and he dived again, carefully, proud of himself.

Soon the biggest of the boys poised himself, shot down into the water, and did not come up. The others stood about, watching. Jerry, after waiting for the sleek brown head to appear, let out a yell of warning; they looked at him idly and turned their eyes back towards the water. After a long time, the boy came up on the other side of a big dark rock, letting the air out of his lungs in a sputtering gasp and a shout of triumph. Immediately, the rest of them dived in. One moment the morning seemed full of chattering boys; the next, the air and the surface of the water were empty. But through the heavy blue, dark shapes could be seen moving and groping.

Jerry dived, shot past the school of underwater swimmers, saw a black wall of rock looming at him, touched it, and bobbed up at once to the surface, where the wall was a low barrier he could see across. There was no one visible; under him, in the water, the dim shapes of the swimmers had disappeared. Then one and then another of the boys came up on the far side of the barrier of rock, and he understood that they had swum through some gap or hole in it. He plunged down again. He could see nothing through the stinging salt water but the blank rock. When he came up, the boys were all on the diving rock, preparing to attempt the feat again. And now, in a panic of failure, he yelled up, in English: 'Look at me! Look!' and he began splashing and kicking in the water like a foolish dog.

They looked down gravely, frowning. He knew the frown. At moments of failure, when he clowned to claim his mother's attention, it was with just this grave, embarrassed inspection that she rewarded him. Through his hot shame, feeling the pleading grin on his face like a scar that he could never remove, he looked up at the group of big brown boys on the rock and shouted: '*Bonjour! Merci! Au revoir! Monsieur, monsieur!*' while he hooked his fingers round his ears and waggled them.

Water surged into his mouth; he choked, sank, came up. The rock, lately weighted with boys, seemed to rear up out of the water as their weight was removed. They were flying down past him, now, into the water; the air was full of falling bodies. Then the rock was empty in the hot sunlight. He counted one, two, three. . . .

At fifty he was terrified. They must all be drowning beneath him, in the watery caves of the rock! At a hundred he stared around him at the empty hillside, wondering if he should yell for help. He counted faster, faster, to hurry them up, to bring them to the surface quickly, to drown them quickly—anything rather than the terror of counting on and on into the blue emptiness of the morning. And then, at a hundred and sixty, the water beyond the rock was full of boys blowing like brown whales. They swam back to the shore without a look at him.

He climbed back to the diving rock and sat down, feeling the hot roughness of it under his thighs. The boys were gathering up their bits of clothing and running off along the shore to another promontory. They were leaving to get away from him. He cried openly, fists in his eyes. There was no one to see him, and he cried himself out.

It seemed to him that a long time had passed, and he swam out to where he could see his mother. Yes, she was still there, a yellow spot under an orange umbrella. He swam back to the big rock, climbed up, and dived into the blue pool among the fanged and angry boulders. Down he went, until he touched the wall of rock again. But the salt was so painful in his eyes that he could not see.

He came to the surface, swam to shore, and went back to the villa to wait for his mother. Soon she walked slowly up the path, swinging her striped bag, the flushed, naked arm dangling beside her. 'I want some swimming goggles,' he panted, defiant and beseeching.

She gave him a patient, inquisitive look as she said casually, 'Well, of course, darling.'

But now, now, now! He must have them this minute, and no other time. He nagged and pestered until she went with him to a shop. As soon as she had bought the goggles, he grabbed them from her hand as if she were going to claim them for herself, and was off, running down the steep path to the bay.

Jerry swam out to the big barrier rock, adjusted the goggles, and dived. The impact of the water broke the rubber-enclosed vacuum, and the goggles came loose. He understood that he must swim down to the base of the rock from the surface of the water. He fixed the goggles tight and firm, filled his lungs, and floated, face down, on the water. Now he could see. It was as if he had eyes of a different kind—fish-eyes that showed everything clear and delicate and wavering in the bright water.

Under him, six or seven feet down, was a floor of perfectly clean, shining white sand, rippled firm and hard by
the tides. Two greyish shapes steered there, like long,
rounded pieces of wood or slate. They were fish. He saw
them nose towards each other, poise motionless, make a dart
forward, swerve off, and come round again. It was like a
water dance. A few inches above them, the water sparkled
as if sequins were dropping through it. Fish again—myriads
of minute fish, the length of his finger-nail, were drifting
through the water, and in a moment he could feel the in-
numerable tiny touches of them against his limbs. It was like
swimming in flaked silver. The great rock the big boys had
swum through rose sheer out of the white sand, black,
tufted lightly with greenish weed. He could see no gap in
it. He swam down to its base.

Again and again he rose, took a big chestful of air, and
went down. Again and again he groped over the surface
of the rock, feeling it, almost hugging it in the desperate need
to find the entrance. And then, once, while he was clinging
to the black wall, his knees came up and he shot his feet out
forward and they met no obstacle. He had found the hole.

He gained the surface, clambered about the stones that
littered the barrier rock until he found a big one, and, with
this in his arms, let himself down over the side of the rock.
he dropped, with the weight, straight to the sandy floor.
Clinging tight to the anchor of stone, he lay on his side and
looked in under the dark shelf at the place where his feet
had gone. He could see the hole. It was an irregular, dark
gap, but he could not see deep into it. He let go of his anchor,
clung with his hands to the edges of the hole, and tried
to push himself in.

He got his head in, found his shoulders jammed, moved them in sidewise, and was inside as far as his waist. He could see nothing ahead. Something soft and clammy touched his mouth, he saw a dark frond moving against the greyish rock, and panic filled him. He thought of octopuses, of clinging weed. He pushed himself out backward and caught a glimpse, as he retreated, of a harmless tentacle of seaweed drifting in the mouth of the tunnel. But it was enough. He reached the sunlight, swam to shore, and lay on the diving rock. He looked down in the blue well of water. He knew he must find his way through that cave, or hole, or tunnel, and out the other side.

First, he thought, he must learn to control his breathing. He let himself down into the water with another big stone in his arms, so that he could lie effortlessly on the bottom of the sea. He counted. One, two, three. He counted steadily. He could hear the movement of blood in his chest. Fifty-one, fifty-two . . . His chest was hurting. He let go of the rock and went up into the air. He saw that the sun was low. He rushed to the villa and found his mother at her supper. She said only 'Did you enjoy yourself?' and he said 'Yes.'

All night the boy dreamed of the water-filled cave in the rock, and as soon as breakfast was over he went to the bay.

That night his nose bled badly. For hours he had been underwater, learning to hold his breath, and now he felt weak and dizzy. His mother said, 'I shouldn't overdo things, darling, if I were you.'

That day and the next, Jerry exercised his lungs as if everything, the whole of his life, all that he would become, depended upon it. And again his nose bled at night, and his mother insisted on his coming with her the next day. It was a torment to him to waste a day of his careful self-training, but he stayed with her on that other beach, which now seemed a place for small children, a place where his mother might lie safe in the sun. It was not his beach.

He did not ask for permission, on the following day, to go to his beach. He went, before his mother could consider the complicated rights and wrongs of the matter. A day's rest, he discovered, had improved his count by ten. The big boys had made the passage while he counted a hundred and sixty. He had been counting fast, in his fright. Probably now, if he tried, he could get through that long tunnel, but he was not going to try yet. A curious, most unchildlike persistence, a controlled impatience, made him wait. In the meantime, he lay underwater on the white sand, littered now by stones he had brought down from the upper air, and studied the entrance to the tunnel. He knew every jut and corner of it, as far as it was possible to see. It was as if he already felt its sharpness about his shoulders.

He sat by the clock in the villa, when his mother was not near, and checked his time. He was incredulous and then proud to find he could hold his breath without strain for two minutes. The words 'two minutes', authorized by the clock, brought the adventure that was so necessary to him close.

In another four days, his mother said casually one morning, they must go home. On the day before they left, he would do it. He would do it if it killed him, he said defiantly to himself. But two days before they were to leave —a day of triumph when he increased his count by fifteen —his nose bled so badly that he turned dizzy and had to lie limply over the big rock like a bit of seaweed, watching

the thick red blood flow on to the rock and trickle slowly
down to the sea. He was frightened. Supposing he turned
dizzy in the tunnel? Supposing he died there, trapped?
Supposing—his head went round, in the hot sun, and he
almost gave up. He thought he would return to the house
and lie down, and next summer, perhaps, when he had
another year's growth in him—*then* he would go through
the hole.

But even after he had made the decision, or thought he
had, he found himself sitting up on the rock and looking
down into the water, and he knew that now, this moment,
when his nose had only just stopped bleeding, when his
head was still sore and throbbing—this was the moment
when he would try. If he did not do it now, he never would.
He was trembling with fear that he would not go, and he
was trembling with horror at that long, long tunnel under
the rock, under the sea. Even in the open sunlight the barrier
rock seemed very wide and very heavy; tons of rock pressed
down on where he would go. If he died there he would lie
until one day—perhaps not before next year—those big
boys would swim into it and find it blocked.

He put on his goggles, fitted them tight, tested the
vacuum. His hands were shaking. Then he chose the biggest
stone he could carry and slipped over the edge of the rock
until half of him was in the cool, enclosing water and half
in the hot sun. He looked up once at the empty sky, filled
his lungs once, twice, and then sank fast to the bottom with
the stone. He let it go and began to count. He took the edges
of the hole in his hands and drew himself into it, wriggling
his shoulders in sideways as he remembered he must,
kicking himself along with his feet.

Soon he was clear inside. He was in a small rock-bound hole filled with yellowish-grey water. The water was pushing him up against the roof. The roof was sharp and pained his back. He pulled himself along with his hands—fast, fast—and used his legs as levers. His head knocked against something; a sharp pain dizzied him. Fifty, fifty-one, fifty-two . . . He was without light, and the water seemed to press upon him with the weight of rock. Seventy-one, seventy-two . . . There was no strain on his lungs. He felt like an inflated balloon, his lungs were so light and easy, but his head was pulsing.

He was being continually pressed against the sharp roof, which felt slimy as well as sharp. Again he thought of octo-puses, and wondered if the tunnel might be filled with weed that could tangle him. He gave himself a panicky, convulsive kick forward, ducked his head, and swam. His feet and hands moved freely, as if in open water. The hole must have widened out. He thought he must be swimming fast, and he was frightened of banging his head if the tunnel narrowed.

A hundred, a hundred and one . . . The water paled. Victory filled him. His lungs were beginning to hurt. A few more strokes and he would be out. He was counting wildly; he said a hundred and fifteen, and then, a long time later, a hundred and fifteen again. The water was a clear jewel-green all around him. Then he saw, above his head, a crack running up through the rock. Sunlight was falling through it, showing the clean dark rock of the tunnel, a single mussel shell, and darkness ahead.

He was at the end of what he could do. He looked up at the crack as if it were filled with air and not water, as if he could put his mouth to it to draw in air. A hundred and fifteen, he heard himself say inside his head—but he had said that long ago. He must go on into the blackness ahead, or he would drown. His head was swelling, his lungs cracking. A hundred and fifteen, a hundred and fifteen pounded through his head, and he feebly clutched at rocks in the dark, pulling himself forward, leaving the brief space of sunlit water behind. He felt he was dying. He was no longer quite conscious. He struggled on in the darkness between lapses into unconsciousness. An immense, swelling pain filled his head, and then the darkness cracked with an explosion of green light. His hands, groping forward, met nothing, and his feet, kicking back, propelled him out into the open sea.

He drifted to the surface, his face turned up to the air. He was gasping like a fish. He felt he would sink now and drown; he could not swim the few feet back to the rock. Then he was clutching it and pulling himself up on to it. He lay face down, gasping. He could see nothing but a red-veined, clotted dark. His eyes must have burst, he thought; they were full of blood. He tore off his goggles and a gout of blood went into the sea. His nose was bleeding, and the blood had filled the goggles.

He scooped up handfuls of water from the cool, salty sea, to splash on his face, and did not know whether it was blood or salt water he tasted. After a time, his heart quieted, his eyes cleared, and he sat up. He could see the local boys, diving and playing half a mile away. He did not want them. He wanted nothing but to get back home and lie down.

In a short while, Jerry swam to shore and climbed slowly up the path to the villa. He flung himself on his bed and slept, waking at the sound of feet on the path outside. His mother was coming back. He rushed to the bathroom, thinking she must not see his face with bloodstains, or tearstains, on it. He came out of the bathroom and met her as she walked into the villa, smiling, her eyes lighting up.

'Have a nice morning?' she asked, laying her hand on his warm brown shoulder a moment.

'Oh, yes, thank you,' he said.

'You look a bit pale.' And then, sharp and anxious, 'How did you bang your head?'

'Oh, just banged it,' he told her.

She looked at him closely. He was strained. His eyes were glazed-looking. She was worried. And then she said to herself: 'Oh, don't fuss! Nothing can happen. He can swim like a fish.'

They sat down to lunch together.

'Mummy,' he said, 'I can stay under water for two minutes—three minutes, at least.' It came bursting out of him.

'Can you, darling?' she said. 'Well, I shouldn't overdo it. I don't think you ought to swim any more today.'

She was ready for a battle of wills, but he gave in at once. It was no longer of the least importance to go to the bay.

NADINE GORDIMER

A Present for a Good Girl

ON AN afternoon in September a woman came into the
jeweller's shop. The two assistants, whose bodies had con-
trived, as human bodies doggedly will, to adapt the straight,
hard stretch of the glass showcases to a support, sagged, hips
thrust forward, elbows leaning in upon their black *crêpe-de-
Chine*-covered stomachs, and looked at her without a flicker,
waiting for her to go. For they could see that she did not
belong there. No woman in a frayed and shapeless old Leghorn hat, carrying a bulging crash shopping-bag, decorated
in church bazaar fashion with wool embroidery, and wearing stained old sandshoes and cheap thick pink stockings that
concertinaed round her ankles, could belong in the jeweller's
shop. They knew the kind; simple, a bit dazed, short-sighted,
and had wandered in mistaking it for the chemist's two
doors up. She would peer round stupidly, looking as if
she had stumbled into Aladdin's cave, and when she saw
the handsome canteens of cutlery, with their beautifully
arranged knives spread like a flashing keyboard in their velvet
beds, and the pretty little faces of the watches in their satin
cases, and the cool, watery preening of the cut glass beneath
its special light, she would mumble and shamble herself out
again. So they stood, unmoved, waiting for her to go.

But, uncomfortably, she didn't go. She advanced right in, half defiantly, half ingratiatingly—she gave a little sniff to herself as if to say: Come on, now! Well, why *shouldn't* I— and put the shopping-bag down on the counter. Then she gave the hat a pull, and stood waiting, not looking at the young ladies.

But still they did not move. Their half-closed eyes rested with faint interest upon the crash shopping-bag, as upon some fossil discovery.

The third assistant, who was sitting at a table threading wedding rings in order on a velvet rod, pushed the rings aside and got up, thinking, with as much crossness as lethargy could muster, 'Well, someone must see what the old creature wants.'

'Yes?' she said.

It was all ready in the woman's mouth; as a child comes threshing up out of water with bulging cheeks, and lets out all its mouthful of breathlessness and enthusiasm in one great gasp, she said: 'Good afternoon, miss, there's a green bag in the window, miss—in the corner, right down near the front. I want to get one for my daughter, she's always talking about a green one—and I wondered, you see, it's really only for Christmas, but I thought . . .'—and her pupils, that seemed to swim like weak small fish in the colourless wetness of her eyes with their underlids drooping down in a reddish peak, darted wildly. Like a beggar exhibiting valuable sores, she smiled on a mouth of gaps and teeth worn like splinters of driftwood.

'You want the green handbag in the window?' asserted the assistant, looking up, then down.

'Well, how much is it?' said the woman, in the coy tone of a confessed secret, screwing up one eye.

But the young assistant would not be drawn into such intimacy.

'I'll have a look . . . ' she said, resigned to wasting her time, and came out from behind the counter. Slow and measured, she unfastened the window catches, leaned in, and drew out the bag. The old woman pressed forward over the counter, her tongue feeling anxiously along the dark canyons of her teeth. She leaned on her elbow and her left hand, with the bones and great knobs that punctuated each joint sliding beneath tough slack skin like that of a tortoise, had taken up a curious pose, hanging indolent from the wrist, like the hand of a Louis XVI dandy pinching up snuff. 'Mmm,' she said, fumbling the air round the bag, wanting to touch it. She breathed hard down her nose, and whilst the assistant parted the bright locked fangs of the zipper and felt for the price-tag inside, the girl held her breath against the fusty sourness of the old woman's breath.

'Four-fifteen,' said the assistant at last.

'Four-fifteen, four-fifteen,' nodded the woman, sucking in her lower lip.

'Ninety-five shillings,' said the assistant, hand on hip.

'Ah,' said the woman, lifting her eyebrows under the flop of the zany hat, as if that explained away any difficulty. 'It's got a mirror?' she asked.

'Yes,' said the assistant ironically. You can't afford it, said the hand on her hip.

'Oh, I'm sure she'll like it,' chatted the woman, fidgeting with the pockets and gadgets of the leather interior. 'She loves green, you know. Everythink must be green. All her dresses and everythink. When I tell her it's supposed to be

unlucky, she just says, "Mum, you're old-fashioned." She's
always wanted a green bag. . . .'

'Then you should certainly take it for her, madam,' said
the assistant. Another minute or two and the old thing
would be gone, muttering she'd see . . . she'd speak to her
husband. . . .

'You see, I thought I'd get it for her for Christmas,' said
the woman. She played with the knobbly string of yellow
beads that stood up like boulders on the bony plateau of her
chest.

'Yes, better take it when you see it.' Habit prompted the
assistant. 'It might be gone, if you wait. You can put it
away till Christmas.'

'Oh well, I couldn't take it *now*—' she said. 'You see I
haven't got the money on me now.'

'Well, we could put it aside for you until tomorrow,' said
the assistant.

The woman stood blinking at her subserviently, with the
smirk of cunning innocence worn by the beggar whilst you
read his tattered 'testimonial'. 'You see, dear,' she said in a
hushed small voice, 'I thought perhaps you'd let me pay for
it, like.' Her face was drawn into a question.

'Can't do that, Miss Pierce,' chimed in the other two
assistants at once, like the representatives of some great
power waking up halfway through a conference in time to
boom a veto on some mewling little voice they haven't
even heard. 'Mr Cano isn't in.'

'You see, the manager isn't in at the moment,' offered the
assistant.

'Oh, I don't expect you to let me *take* it,' protested the
woman, smiling at the young ladies as if they had just done

her the most charming favour. 'I just wanted to pay some-think down on it, then you could keep it here for me, and I'd come in every week and pay somethink more off it.'

She grinned at them all like a cornered urchin.

'I see,' said the girl Miss Pierce, not prepared for this.

'You can't do it without Mr Cano's permission,' stated the other two. 'You can't do it without him.'

'All right, all right, I know,' said Miss Pierce. 'How much did you want to pay now?' she asked the woman.

Subdued with tension, the old creature grappled down in the shopping-bag and dragged up a thin purse. 'I could let you have ten bob,' she said.

'And how long to pay the balance?'

'Well, until Chr—until just about the fifteenth of December.'

'It's out of the question, Miss Pierce,' said one of the others in a high voice.

The girl heard it behind her; in front of her the old woman grinned on her bad teeth, like a dog continuing to wag its tail even at the person who approaches to take away the bone that enchants it.

'All right,' said the girl suddenly.

Silently the woman took a ten-shilling note from the flat stomach of her purse, and waited in silence whilst the receipt was made out. The moment she had the receipt in her possession, and was folding it away in the purse and the purse away in the crash bag, a mood of lighthearted talka-tiveness seized her. She opened up into confidential matey-ness like a Japanese paper flower joyously pretending to be a flower instead of a bit of paper as it swells with water.

She spoke only of her daughter. What her daughter always said, and what she always told her daughter.

'You must know my daughter—' she said, pooh-poohing the remote notion that the girl mightn't. '*You know*, dear, she's the cashier at the Grand Lyceum—fair girl, got a very good figure . . . ?'—She had a peculiar way of speaking; each 'd' was a little step before which her voice hesitated, then hastily tripped over.

'Yes,' murmured Miss Pierce, who was actually quite a frequent patron of the cinema in question, but who was never reduced to buying her own seat, and so had never seen the cashier. 'Yes, I think I have seen——'

'Wears a lot of green? Got a quiet way of talking?' went on the woman. 'Of course you know her. It's a good job, you know. She's a clever girl—sharp as a needle. She's been a good daughter to me, I must say. Not like some. That's why I'm glad I got that bag for her. She's been wanting a green one for a long time; I seen her, when we've been walking along, stopping to look in the shop window. And when I've asked her, she's said, no, nothin', just looking generally. But I knew what it was all right; sure enough, somewhere in the window there was always bound to be a green bag. . . .'

When she had shambled out with her flattened heels leaning over the sides of the old sandshoes, the two assistants stood looking at Miss Pierce. 'Well, don't say *we* said it was all right. You know Mr Cano——'

'Peculiar-looking woman,' reproached the other one. 'Did you see the way she was dressed! She looks to me as if she drinks, too.'

'Well, why don't you ever do anything, anyway? Why

do you always wait for me to come forward?' flashed out Miss Pierce, in a sudden temper.

*

Two weeks went by and then the woman came in, with an air of wanting to get her ten-shilling note safely paid in before it 'went' on other things. She asked to see the bag again, and repeated to her fellow conspirator, Miss Pierce, the details of her daughter's taste, colour preferences, and mental powers. To get rid of the woman, the girl pretended to have taken particular note of the fair-haired cashier the last evening she had visited the Grand Lyceum. The mother became almost speechless with an excess of quiet pride: she seemed to go off into a sort of dream, leaning on the counter, saying very low, 'Yes, I'd like to see her face on Christmas morning . . . I'd like to see her face . . . That I would. . . .' Putting away her second receipt with the greatest of care, she went slowly out of the shop, as if she were walking straight off the edge of a cloud.

'Funny old stick,' said Miss Pierce, writing 'Balance, £3 15s.' on the parcel.

The next time the woman came in she was embarrassingly garrulous, and insisted on offering Miss Pierce a cigarette from an enamelled tin case picturing two yellow cockatoos and fastened with a catch which was evidently rather tricky because she fumbled such a long time over getting it open. Under the same frayed Leghorn hat, she looked queerer than ever; her face was stiff, as if carefully balanced, and there was a streak of mauvish lipstick on her mouth. She paid only five shillings, with profuse apologies: 'As God's my witness,

I'll pay the lot off at the beginning of the month,' she said loudly, raising her right hand. 'As God's my witness . . .' Her hand dropped and suddenly she smiled, sweetly, sweetly. 'For my little girl . . . my little girl,' she whispered, evidently to herself. Poor Miss Pierce smiled back fiercely in embarrassment. And suddenly the woman was gone.

The third time she came it was in the morning, and it seemed to the young Miss Pierce that the woman was really much older than she had noticed: she walked so falteringly, the crash shopping-bag was much too heavy for her, and her eyes looked red in her bluish-pale face. Had she been crying, perhaps? Miss Pierce thought perhaps the poor old thing had to work very hard at housework; there was a faint smell of methylated spirit about her—she must have been cleaning windows. Four-pounds-fifteen! Why, it must be a fortune to her! Miss Pierce wondered if a peroxide-blonde cashier from the Grand Lyceum was worthy of it. Anyway, the green handbag was another fifteen shillings nearer being paid for.

And that, it seemed, was as far as it would ever get.

Weeks went by, and the woman did not appear; Miss Pierce hid the bag away from the business-like eyes of Mr Cano. 'What's this?' he would say. '*How* long—?—Put it back into stock. Return the woman's deposit to her. . . .' So the green bag lay waiting behind a pile of hand-tooled leather writing-cases.

An intoxication of buying grew upon the town as every day Christmas moved up a notch nearer, and soon the three assistants were elbowing one another out of the way as they smiled, persuaded, suggested, to the timorous, the vacillating, the imperious who came to buy. Miss Pierce really did

not even have time to wonder if the woman would come for
the bag; her shop-girl's attention was already wrangled into
half a dozen divisions by half a dozen equally demanding
customers as it was; there was no small shred left that was
not immediately snatched up by someone who had been
waiting fully three-quarters of an hour to see a tortoise-shell
powder-bowl.

But in the fine high frenzy of half past four on the last
Saturday afternoon before Christmas, Miss Pierce was inter-
rupted. 'Your customer's here'—one of the other two
young ladies prodded her elbow. '—What?' said the girl,
dodging the blinding demand of eyes. 'The green handbag,'
said the other, smiling with great brilliance, and diving back.

The harassed girl dodged in and out to the other side of
the shop. In the dazed preoccupation that results as a kind of
spiritual sunstroke from over-exposure to the question and
demand of a daylong crowd, she could not recall any green
handbag. But then she saw the woman in the battered
garden-party Leghorn standing just within the doorway,
and of course!—the green handbag, £2 15s. balance, behind
the writing-cases. She went forward with a quick smile.

'S'ere . . .' said the woman, handing out a pound note as
if to a blank wall. ' 'F you've sorl tha bag t'anyone . . . I
pay'dfirit and you've got norite t'crooka poorwoman.'—
Her voice whined through the persuasive buzz of the shop.
Harsh fumes surrounded her as rising incense round some
image.

Miss Pierce looked at her in astonishment.

Dropping the crash bag, the woman turned to look at it,
lying on the floor, as if it were some animal that had just
crawled to her feet. She tried to pick it up, but could not.

Half bent to the floor, she looked up at Miss Pierce with a
sudden chuckle, like a naughty child.

Miss Pierce stood quite still.

'Why'd'you keepm'waiting, whydonchu giviterme,' said
the woman with great dignity. There was a red poppy, the
kind that charitable organizations give away on collection
days, pinned on to the brim of the hat with a large safety-pin.

Miss Pierce trembled like a trapped rabbit.

'Youdonwana be'fraiduvme,' said the woman with a
sudden cunning flash of understanding. 'Sorry . . .' She
wagged her head. 'Sorry . . .'

Miss Pierce burned with guilt. 'I'll just get—I mean, I'll
see . . .' she tried.

'Musn be'fraid uvaporeolwoman. Iwan the—the—bag'—
she stopped and thought hard—'the-the *green* bag I got f'my
daughter. Y'know mydaughter?' she urged, clutching
Miss Pierce's arm. ''Course y'know mydaughter—' She
stopped and smiled, closing her eyes. 'S'ere,' she said,
putting down the pound note.

'But that's not enough,' said Miss Pierce very loudly,
as if talking to a deaf person. 'Not enough. You owe
two-pounds-fifteen on the bag'—holding up two fingers—
'Two-pounds-fifteen.'

'Wha's sat?' said the woman, stupidly. Her face grew
woeful, sullen. 'Don wanagiviterme. Y'don wanagiviterme.'

'But you haven't paid for it, you see,' said Miss Pierce
miserably. Mr Cano was frowning at her through the crowd;
she could sense his one twitching eyebrow, questioning.

'Howmuchwasit?' whispered the woman, winking at her
and leaning over into her face.

'Four-pounds-fifteen. You remember.'

'Wasit?' she giggled. 'Wasit?'

'You have to pay another pound and fifteen shillings.'

The woman knelt on the floor and felt down amongst the lumps and bulges of the crash shopping-bag, collapsed on its side on the floor. At last she got up again. Some anchor in the heart that even the vast swelling uncharted seas of drunkenness could not free her of, pulled at her. Underneath her stiff face, her glassed-out eyes, it was horrible to see that she was alive and struggling. The silliness of being drunk would not come up to save her.

'Iwaned to getit for her,' she said. 'I *mean* t'getit for her.'

The broken brim of the hat hid her face as she felt her way out. The whole shop was watching, each man from the pinnacle of his own self-triumph.

It had hardly turned back to its own business again when a pale girl, violently white-faced, with the thin pale hair of a slum child, swept trembling into the shop. She stood there leaning forward on her toes, shuddering with anger. Just behind her, held leashed by the terrible look of her eye, was the old woman, open-mouthed. The girl's eyes searched desperately round the shop. They seemed to draw Miss Pierce out from behind the counter: she came slowly forward. A flash of angry disgust passed from the girl to the old woman, who blinked beneath it as from a whip.

'Now what is it?' blurted the girl. 'What does she owe here?'

'She's paid some, you see,' ventured Miss Pierce. They were like doctors in discussion over the patient's prone body.

'Tell me how much, and I'll pay it,' the girl cut in violently. Under the pale spare skin of her neck, her heart flew up madly, as a bird dashing again and again at its cage.

'Oh, it's all right,' faltered Miss Pierce, avoiding looking at the old woman. 'She's not so very much behind in her payments. It's not absolutely necessary that she take the bag now.'

Hot bright tears at the recollection of some recent angry scene fevered the girl's eyes. '*Tell me how much it is,*' she whispered fiercely, crazily. She swallowed her tears. '*She* can't pay,' she said, with a look of hopeless disgust at the old woman.

'The bag was four-pounds-fifteen. She owes one-fifteen on it.'

'A bag for four-pounds-fifteen,' said the girl bitterly, so overwhelmed by a fresh welling of furious despair and irritation that her pale eyes filled with bright tears again. She turned and looked at the old woman; her hand sank leaden at her side, as if defeated in the desire to strike. 'What next? Always something. Some rubbish. Now a bag. What for—? You people give her things. She's not responsible. I've had just about enough of it.—She ought to be in a home, she should. I can't stand it any longer.' The old woman looked out at her from under her eyelids.

Trembling, the girl jerked out one pound and fifteen shillings in silver and gave it up with a gesture of hopeless impotence to Miss Pierce. Miss Pierce handed to her the parcel containing the green handbag. The girl looked at it for a moment, with an expression of quizzical, sullen disgust. She looked as if she would have liked to hurl it away, as far as her arm could. Then she picked it up, and went out of the doorway.

'Come on,' she ordered in a low, dead voice.

And the old woman swayed after her out into the street.

GEORGE EWART EVANS

Possessions

———

A MONTH after my father died they sold up the shop to pay the debts. Our big family and the pit-strikes had knocked the stuffing out of the grocery business and after my father's death it passed out without a whimper. The only bit of stock left after the sell-up was the pony and cart. My mother had held on to the pony by swearing it was hers—down in the books in her name; but even then, if she hadn't been pretty downright with the auctioneer, a big chap with a smooth skin and an expensive, whisky complexion, they'd have put the pony under the hammer as well. They left the cart because it wasn't worth taking away. Ma also clung on to the old piano with the pleated silk front. The auctioneer had walked round it, mumbling that it would fetch a pound or two and ought by rights to be sold up with the other things, but Ma had stood her ground over this, too.

Dick, the pony, had been with us for nearly twenty years, and none of us wanted to part with him. He was like one of the family. He was something more than an ordinary pony, too: he had some real blood in him. My uncle bred Welsh cobs and Dick had come from his stable. When he was younger he pulled the grocer's cart as though he was doing us all a big favour. But he had no belly then for this kind of life: there were too many stops in it for his liking, and he waited for the time when he had the light pleasure-trap behind him or our Tom on his back. Then you'd see him prance and tear the road up as you'd expect from a pony whose uncles and cousins had fought in two wars. He stood about thirteen hands, and he could do most things bar talk, and if tossing his head was anything to go by, he'd make a pretty good try at that.

But there was a bit of difference just before the sell-up, when Ma said she was determined to keep the pony. Tom, my eldest brother, tried to reason with her.

'But what are you going to do with the pony, Ma?' he asked.

'What should I be doing with him? Let him rest, of course! He's done his work. Besides, you'll all be growing up before long and going off and getting married and leaving the house. I'd like to have the old pony for a bit of company.'

'Talk sense, Ma,' Tom said. 'Who's talking of leaving you?'

'Well, I'm keeping the pony,' Ma said doggedly, 'and the piano as well. Gomer's got talent, and we can make do with that old piano for a good while yet.'

A short while after the sale Tom had another try to make Ma see reason. The pony was in the stall, just doing nothing except take Gomer and me for a joy-ride in the rickety old cart occasionally

'We'll have to sell Dick,' Tom said one day after he came home from his new job at the pit. 'We can't afford to keep him, Ma. We're short of money.'

My mother went on with her darning, her spectacles halfway down her nose. Then our Gomer spoke: 'Dando

Hamer the Ragman has been asking about Dick,' he said. 'His donkey is failing.' But straightway he wished that he'd not opened his mouth, because he wanted to keep the pony as much as I did.

'Dando Hamer, is it?' Ma said, sitting up. 'There's a fine one to get the pony! He'd either work him to death or else freeze him, keeping him standing outside the Greyhound while he gets drunk. And when he'd slaved him until he was a bag of bones, he'd pack him off to the knacker's yard.'

'Look, Ma,' Tom said persuasively, 'why not have a word with Dando Hamer? I'll ask him to call up, and if he offers a fair price, let him have the pony. Better to sell him to Hamer, where we can keep an eye on him, than for him to go goodness knows where, and get the skin tanned off his backside.' Then he added quietly: 'Don't forget all the oats we'll be having to buy. He's just about through the bin we had left out of the stock.'

My mother could see the sense of Tom's arguments, but she pondered for a long time before answering. Then she laid down her darning. 'All right, you know best, Tom,' she said without looking up. 'We'd better see this Dando and have a talk with him. I'll send Gomer or Willy down to ask him to call. I tell you this, though: the family won't be the same without the pony; it will be like losing one of the children.' Then as a stubborn afterthought: 'But say what you like, I'm going to keep that piano. I saved it from the sale, and I'm going to keep it even if it's the last stick of furniture we've got in the house!'

The next morning I walked down to call on Dando the Ragman; and took the first step towards selling the pony. I felt that I was drawing down heavy shutters on the past.

There never had been a time when I couldn't remember hearing the strangely comforting clatter of the pony's hoofs on the cobbles in the stable; and the way he gave you a prod with his nose or a playful nip on the arm with his teeth when he wanted something you were a bit slow in getting. Nor could I forget the time when I was very young and the business was roaring ahead like a heath-fire, and Dick the pony was lifting up his knees high enough to make a champion trotter look to his rosettes and his ribbons. At that time, when we had made our last call, usually at the topmost house of the village, halfway up the steep hillside, Tom would sit back on an upturned sugar-box with the reins loose in his hands, and he'd say, 'Home, Dick!' and the old pony would go as fast as a baby for his first birthday; his neck arched, his legs working like pistons, and the cart like a flying chariot behind him. I was very sad, and both my feet were on my mother's side in this business of selling the pony. But I could see that the sense was with Tom.

Dando the Ragman lived by himself at the bottom end of the village, in an old stone cottage by the river. When he opened the door to my knock I saw him without his cap for the first time, and I noticed how his hair was all matted and tangled like the inside of an old mattress. His eyes were as red as two plums.

'My mother wants you to call to see the pony,' I said.

Dando's lips moved silently before he spoke. A few of the boys were saying that he had given some of his wits away with the balloons and paper windmills that he traded in exchange for rags. But he seemed to have a sure grip on all of his wits this morning. 'Selling him, she is?' His eyes narrowed as he thrust his bristle-covered face towards me.

'I don't know,' I answered cautiously, mistrusting the cunning bloodshot eyes.

He grinned as he thrust a two-inch nail through the top of his trousers to secure one tag of his braces. 'That will be all right, boy. Tell her I'll call this morning.' And as I walked back towards the village he roared after me in his raucous street-cry: 'And if you've got any old rags or jam-jars, false-teeth or ironwork, turn 'em out, turn 'em out! Dando'll be there!' I hurried off up the road, glad to be away from this apparition who was likely soon to be Dick's new owner.

Dando came up to our house later that morning, just after Gomer and I had got home from school. Gomer was prac-tising on the piano, and Dando stood at the back door looking through to the parlour at him and listening, as though he were in a trance, to the old notes' chiming. Ma paused by the table and watched Dando for a moment. Then she clicked her tongue in disgust and whispered: 'Drunk already, at this time of the morning!' Gomer's left hand stuttered a bit and he came to a stop. The spell was broken, and Dando collected himself and nodded at Ma, whom he had noticed now for the first time. Ma told him about the pony.

'But I'm not wanting a pony, Mrs Pritchard,' he said, looking sheepishly at her from under his peaked cap. Dando was a bit afraid of Ma's dark eyes and her sharp tongue.

'Well, there's not much use you and me talking by here, is there?' Ma said briskly, taking off her apron. Dando leaned against the jamb of the door and scratched the back of his neck. He watched her fold her apron and place it neatly on the dresser. He was still silent after she had smoothed down her skirt in a last gesture. She repeated: 'If you don't want the pony, there's no use our wasting breath, is there now?'

Dando seemed to ponder this. Then he stood up off the door-jamb and scratched his shoulder. He spoke quietly, cautiously, like a pleading child, uncertain of the effect of his words: 'Any rags today, Mrs Pritchard, jars, old iron-work, false——'

'No!'

He took off his cap, examined the inside of it carefully, and clapped it back on his head. 'How old would your pony be now, Mrs Pritchard?' he asked casually, as though it was a question he had just read in the dirty lining of his cap.

'Nineteen,' Ma answered boldly, waving Gomer and me back to give Dando air to make up his mind.

'A bit old for a horse,' he answered with a wary, tentative leer at Ma.

'Old! Nonsense! Be off with you! This pony's father fought in the wars and lived until he was thirty-one. He used to carry a thirteen-stone drunken farmer over the mountains to Pentre until a few years before he died. If you think he's old,' she took up the folded apron and held it under Dando's nose, 'you try stopping him once he's got his head pointed towards home.'

'Can I see the pony, Mrs Pritchard?' Dando asked, very subdued.

'Certainly, if you're thinking of buying him. Otherwise it will be a waste of my time.' She pretended to hesitate, then said, 'Besides, I've not decided for sure that I'm going to sell him.'

But Ma showed him the pony; and Dando was made to

feel that he was looking at a prince among horses, a possession without price; and indeed he was, but only to my
mother. They manœuvred and haggled for half an hour,
until at last Dando offered a pound less than the eight Ma
had asked for him. Ma accepted the offer and the skirmish
was over.

Afterwards, Tom said that it was a good price, better
than we should have got elsewhere. But she said, 'Fair price
or no, I wouldn't let him take the pony from the stable until
he'd sworn, with his five fingers to the sky, that he'd
treat him kindly and never let the knackers get hold of him
while he was still living.'

After the pony had gone, the empty stall was like a big
draughty hole in the side of the house. Dando Hamer had
sold his donkey, and Dick was now in the shafts of the rag-
and-bone cart, though none of us had seen him yet. Whenever we heard Dando's war-cry bellowing up the street,
Gomer and I slunk into the house, not wishing to see Dick
heading Dando's sordid turnout.

But we still had the piano; and Ma polished it so often
that it shone better than a pulpit; and our Gomer, as he sat
by it, could see the top of the garden and the post for the
clothes-line reflected in it. Badgered by Ma, Gomer practised
night and morning; and at no time was the house free, or so
it seemed, from the tinkling chimes of 'The Bells of Aberdovey'.

*

Within a few weeks, in the press of the new order after
the sale, the pony slipped out of my mind. But my mother

still had him very much in mind all the time. As soon as she heard the ragman's raucous voice in the street she'd be out on the doorstep to see how the pony was shaping. One day she walked across to him with an apple. Dick knew her as soon as she approached, and he lifted his head and showed a little of his old spirit. Ma was surprised, as we were, when she saw Dick close up—not that there was anything wrong with him, not anything you could put your finger on. Although he was a good deal thinner, he was still in pretty good condition. Yet he seemed to have shrunk into himself; his head had lost its angle and his neck its arch. He reminded you of an old man who had reached the breathing-through-the-mouth stage. Ma's eyes darkened as she drew her hands through the pony's mane. Often when she was moved by some emotion it turned suddenly to anger; and now she looked at Dando and sharpened her tongue: 'You want to use the brush and currycomb on this pony a bit more than you're doing!' Harmless words, but spoken in a voice and with a look that accused Dando of a crime no less than the starving of his own children would have been. His bloodshot eyes looked obliquely at her from under the peak of his cap; but that morning he didn't have the spirit in him to say that the pony was no longer hers.

A short while after this a sore developed on one of the pony's legs. Ma spotted it and told Dando that she would report him unless he got the leg attended to. The sore got better, but it was plain that the pony was being neglected. Dando spent all his time in the pubs. He'd start out early on his round, full of good intentions as a new minister; and then he'd stop at the Greyhound and get himself anchored there for the rest of the day with the old pony drooping his head outside. Tom used to see him there often as he came home from work in the afternoon; but he told Ma nothing.

One evening, however, we could see that something was wrong. It had been a pouring wet day, with a cold wind blowing the weather up the valley. Tom's face was black even after he'd washed all the coal off it. As he was having his meal, he broke a piece of bread savagely and nodded his head over his shoulder as he blurted out: 'That pony's outside the Greyhound in this rain. Looks as if he's been there all day.'

Ma returned the teapot to the hob and looked at Tom. She took her apron off and folded it neatly on the dresser. Something was going to happen.

'Go outside to the stable, Gomer,' she ordered. 'There's still a lot of bracken in the loft. Strew it deep in Dick's stall.'

'What are you going to do, Ma?' Tom asked.

'We're going to have him back.'

'But you can't!'

'Can't we?' she said, looking round for her coat. 'We'll see! I'll go for him myself if no one else will.'

'But you can't, Ma! It would be stealing to fetch him back here.'

'Who's talking about stealing? He's outside the Greyhound, is he?'

'Ay, tied to the fence at the side.'

'Well, you've only got to loosen him!' Ma said, her dark eyes dancing with anger, 'and I know which home he'll make for!'

It was as simple as that, and none of us had thought about it! Tom got up from the table and reached for his cap. Ma said: 'No, let one of the boys go, Tom. It won't look so . . .

downright,' she added cunningly. 'You go, Willy,' she said, turning to me. 'It's still raining hard, so the streets will be empty. Just untie him and stand back. Here, take this sugar with you.'

I was outside on the pavement in no time, with a pocket-ful of lump-sugar and my face red with excitement. It was raining sheets of glass, and the pony was almost frozen when I got down to him. He head was as low as the ground. The road was a stream and the street was deserted. As I gave him the sugar, I spoke his name. He nudged me in his old way, and tried to get his nose into my pocket. 'Now he's alive,' I thought, 'and now he'll go.' I slipped the piece of orange-box rope off his bit; and the street was still empty as he turned his head round to the road. Then I said, 'Home, Dick!'

The old pony turned his head and looked at me inquir-ingly. I repeated the words. His ears went up suddenly—and within a few seconds the wheels of the rag-cart were turning faster than the wheels of a pit-cage. And all the rags and cans Dando had collected before he'd gone to earth were strew-ing themselves about the swimming roadway. Up the street went the pony, the cart flying behind him and fanning out the water like a speedboat. Ma was right: he'd find his way home; and, what's more, he'd be there in half of no time. But Gomer and Tom were there waiting for him, and when I got home he was deep and snug in his bracken with a feed of oats in the manger.

After the excitement of the transfer was over we went back to the kitchen. Tom said: 'What are we going to do now, Ma? Hamer'll be up as soon as he's sober. What are we going to tell him?'

'Tell him he can't have the pony.'

Tom looked worried: 'But he bought him, Ma!'

'Ay, but he didn't keep his part of the bargain.'

'He won't take that for an answer, daft as he is.'

'He needn't. I'm going to buy Dick back from him.'

'Buy him! But what are you going to use for money?'

'I'll get the money. We'll sell the piano.'

'But what about our Gomer's music-lessons?'

'Gomer can learn the flute. Can't you Gomer?' she asked, turning to my youngest brother with persuasion ready on the tip of her tongue. But Gomer nodded: he was easy; he wouldn't pout over the loss of the piano. In any case he'd got no further than 'The Bells of Aberdovey', and his left hand was shaky even with those.

*

Dando Hamer came up early next morning and Ma was ready for him. Gomer and I were there to see the fun. Dando was very mild and sheepish.

''Morning, Mrs Pritchard,' he said. 'Thank you for putting up the pony.' Ma looked at him without speaking, and he twirled the peak of his cap uneasily. 'It was all a perfect accident,' he went on quite animatedly. 'I was detained, you see, longer than I expected.'

'Dando Hamer,' Ma said with all the scorn she could command, 'you're not fit to brush out the pony's stall!'

Dando bent his head and acknowledged his failings. 'Can I have him now?' he asked after a few long seconds.

Ma quietly folded her apron: 'No, you cannot. The pony is staying with me,' she said.

Dando stiffened and worked himself into a fury. A flood

of words poured out, all in a beery jumble. The word *police* was mixed up with them.

'Police!' my mother said quietly. 'Don't you use that word, Dando. Just you be thinking what you'll say when I've fetched the Cruelty Inspector to see the pony!'

Dando worked his lips in silence. 'But how can I go on my round?' he whined.

'Davy Prothero Bonanza Stores has just bought a motor-car, and his horse is spare. Go up and ask him to lend you the horse, and take your old cart away from here. I'll pay back the money you gave me for the pony.'

Dando looked narrowly at my mother. He knew that there were no long stockings hidden in our house. 'When, Mrs Pritchard?' he asked with a polite leer.

'As soon as I've sold the piano. Be off with you now! I can't waste time talking to no purpose.'

But Dando had suddenly brightened up. The word *piano* had struck a hidden chord somewhere deep inside him. 'Is that the piano with the green front?' he asked eagerly. 'Wanting to sell it you are?'

'Yes!'

'Can I have a look at it?'

My mother stared at Dando, and then she remembered how he'd stood listening at the back door to Gomer's playing when first he had come to the house, weeks ago. She motioned him to follow her into the parlour. He stood back from the old piano, his cap in his hand and his little mottled eyes dancing under his untidy mop of grey hair. 'Does it still work?' he whispered.

'Of course it works,' Ma answered scornfully. 'Our Gomer can nearly make it sing!'

She moved her finger across the keys, all yellowed with age, and Dando was plainly moved by the tinkling shower of notes that scattered themselves about the room. He stood before the piano as if it were an altar. The melancholy echo of the notes, filling the room long after they had been sounded, had stirred some long-forgotten memory in him. He was a man transformed: a man who had heard angels. Then he stirred to life and blurted out suddenly: 'The pony back, and one pound extra for the piano!'

Ma looked at him and saw his excitement. 'Two pounds with the pony,' she countered.

Dando glanced at the piano again.

'Go on,' Ma encouraged, 'take your time. Have a good look at it!'

He stepped forward timidly and ran his hand over the silk front and touched the smooth mahogany with reverence. His fingers hovered above the keys, but he drew back before striking them. Still looking at the piano, he said: 'Right you are, Mrs Pritchard. A beautiful instrument! Two pounds and the piano. Fetch it before tea-time. Here's the money to start with.' And with one movement he whipped out the two notes from his inside pocket. He placed them on the piano and was away up to Prothero's to get the loan of a horse. Some strange concord of sweet forgotten sounds had moved Dando so that he was already a new man with a shining purpose in life.

Ma smiled as she watched him hurrying away. 'And now the Lord preserve us,' she cried, shaking her head. 'Dando's going to teach himself to play.' And later, as she got Gomer and me a meal, she said: 'I think you'll do better with the flute, Gomer. That old piano was getting out of tune, anyway. A trouble, too, it was getting to polish it every day.'

Dando borrowed Prothero's horse, as Ma had suggested, and fetched the piano that afternoon. And Dick stayed in his old stall and soon had some flesh on his bones again. None of us minded very much about losing the piano. Its tinkling had become as unwelcome as the sound of the school bell; and until Ma could get him a flute Gomer was quite content to play at football. Tom brought home a card-table he'd won in a raffle, and Ma placed it in the parlour to fill up the space; and soon the piano was forgotten.

*

At least so we thought, until a certain morning when Ma went in to polish what was left of the furniture. It was hard to say just what had reminded her of the piano. Perhaps she had heard, as she bent down to her dusting, an echo of one of its chiming, melancholy notes; or perhaps she had just seen its dark outline on the faded wallpaper. Whatever it was, she stopped and called to Gomer and me in the back kitchen: 'I wonder how the piano is getting on. I wonder if that Dando is using it properly. I'll have to take a walk down that way before I'm much older, just to have a look at it. Pity for the damp to get into it and ruin it—a beautiful instrument like that.'

And as I looked at Gomer I saw his face beginning to screw itself up dolefully, exactly as it used to do when he struggled to ring those chiming, jangling 'Bells of Aberdovey'.

JOHN STEINBECK

The Raid

———————

IT WAS dark in the little California town when the two men stepped from the lunch car and strode arrogantly through the back streets. The air was full of the sweet smell of fermenting fruit from the packing plants. High over the corners, blue arc lights swung in the wind and put moving shadows of telephone wires on the ground. The old wooden buildings were silent and resting. The dirty windows dismally reflected the street lights.

The two men were about the same size, but one was much older than the other. Their hair was cropped, they wore blue jeans. The older man had on a peajacket, while the younger wore a blue turtle-neck sweater. As they swung down the dark street, footsteps echoed back loudly from the wooden buildings. The younger man began to whistle 'Come to Me My Melancholy Baby'. He stopped abruptly. 'I wish that damn' tune would get out of my head. It's been going all day. It's an old tune, too.'

His companion turned towards him. 'You're scared, Root. Tell the truth. You're scared as hell.'

They were passing under one of the blue street lights. Root's face put on its toughest look, the eyes squinted, the mouth went crooked and bitter. 'No, I ain't scared.'

They were out of the light. His face relaxed again. 'I wish I knew the ropes bettter. You been out before, Dick. You know what to expect. But I ain't ever been out.'

'The way to learn is to do,' Dick quoted sententiously. 'You never really learn nothing from books.'

They crossed a railroad track. A block tower up the line a little was starred with green lights. 'It's awful dark,' said Root. 'I wonder if the moon will come up later. Usually does when it's so dark. You going to make the first speech, Dick?'

'No, you make it. I had more experience than you. I'll watch them while you talk and then I can smack them where I know they bite. Know what you're going to say?'

'Sure I do. I got it all in my head, every word. I wrote it out and learned it. I heard guys tell how they got up and couldn't think of a thing to say, and then all of a sudden they just started in like it was somebody else, and the words came out like water out of a hydrant. Big Mike Sheane said it was like that with him. But I wasn't taking no chances, so I wrote it out.'

A train hooted mournfully, and in a moment it rounded a bend and pushed its terrible light down the track. The lighted coaches rattled past. Dick turned to watch it go by. 'Not many people on that one,' he said with satisfaction. 'Didn't you say your old man worked on the railroad?'

Root tried to keep the bitterness out of his voice. 'Sure, he works on the road. He's a brakeman. He kicked me out when he found out what I was doing. He was scared he'd lose his job. He couldn't see. I talked to him, but he just couldn't see. He kicked me right out.' Root's voice was lonely. Suddenly he realized how he had weakened and how he sounded homesick. 'That's the trouble with them,' he went on harshly. 'They can't see beyond their jobs. They can't see what's happening to them. They hang on to their chains.'

'Save it,' said Dick. 'That's good stuff. Is that part of your speech?'

'No, but I guess I'll put it in if you say it's good.'

The street lights were fewer now. A line of locust trees grew along the road, for the town was beginning to thin and the country took control. Along the unpaved road there were a few little houses with ill-kept gardens.

'Jesus! It's dark,' Root said again. 'I wonder if there'll be any trouble. It's a good night to get away if anything happens.'

Dick snorted into the collar of his peajacket. They walked along in silence for a while.

'Do you think you'd try to get away, Dick?' Root asked.

'No, by God! It's against orders. If anything happens we got to stick. You're just a kid. I guess you'd run if I let you!'

Root blustered: 'You think you're hell on wheels just because you been out a few times. You'd think you was a hundred to hear you talk.'

'I'm dry behind the ears, anyway,' said Dick.

Root walked with his head down. He said softly: 'Dick, are you sure you wouldn't run? Are you sure you could just stand there and take it?'

'Of course I'm sure. I've done it before. It's the orders, ain't it? Why, it's good publicity.' He peered through the darkness at Root. 'What makes you ask, kid? You scared you'll run? If you're scared you got no business here.'

Root shivered. 'Listen, Dick, you're a good guy. You won't tell nobody what I say, will you? I never been tried. How do I know what I'll do if somebody smacks me in the face with a club? How can anybody tell what he'd do? I don't think I'd run. I'd try not to run.'

'All right, kid. Let it go at that. But you try running, and I'll turn your name in. We got no place for yellow bastards. You remember that, kid.'

'Oh, lay off that kid stuff. You're running that in the ground.'

The locust trees grew closer together as they went. The wind rustled gently in the leaves. A dog growled in one of the yards as the men went by. A light fog began to drift down through the air, and the stars were swallowed in it. 'You sure you got everything ready?' Dick asked. 'Got the lamps? Got the lit'ature? I left all that to you.'

'I did it all this afternoon,' said Root. 'I didn't put the posters up yet, but I got them in a box out there.'

'Got oil in the lamps?'

'They had plenty in. Say, Dick, I guess some bastard has squealed, don't you?'

'Sure. Somebody always squeals.'

'Well, you didn't hear nothing about no raid, did you?'

'How the hell would I hear? You think they'd come and tell me they was going to knock my can off? Get hold of yourself, Root. You got the pants scared off you. You're going to make me nervous if you don't cut it out.'

II

They approached a low, square building, black and heavy in the darkness. Their feet pounded on a wooden sidewalk. 'Nobody here, yet,' said Dick. 'Let's open her up and get some light.' They had come to a deserted store. The old show-windows were opaque with dirt. A Lucky Strike poster was stuck to the glass on one side while a big cardboard Coca-Cola lady stood like a ghost in the other. Dick threw open the double doors and walked in. He struck a match and lighted a kerosene lamp, got the chimney back in place, and set the lamp on an up-ended apple box. 'Come on, Root, we got to get things ready.'

The walls of the building were scabrous with streaked whitewash. A pile of dusty newspapers had been kicked into a corner. The two back windows were laced with cobwebs. Except for three apple boxes, there was nothing at all in the store.

Root walked to one of the boxes and took out a large poster bearing a portrait of a man done in harsh reds and blacks. He tacked the portrait to the whitewashed wall behind the lamp. Then he tacked another poster beside it, a large red symbol on a white background. Last he up-ended another apple box and piled leaflets and little paper-bound books on it. His footsteps were loud on the bare wooden floor. 'Light the other lamp, Dick! It's too damned dark in here.'

'Scared of the dark, too, kid?'

'No. The men will be here pretty soon. We want to have more light when they come. What time is it?'

Dick looked at his watch. 'Quarter to eight. Some of the guys ought to be here pretty soon now.' He put his hands in the breast pockets of his peajacket and stood loosely by the box of pamphlets. There was nothing to sit on. The black and red portrait stared harshly out at the room. Root leaned against the wall.

The light from one of the lamps yellowed, and the flame

slowly sank down. Dick stepped over to it. 'I thought you said there was plenty of oil. This one's dry.'

'I thought there was plenty. Look! The other one's nearly full. We can pour some of that oil in this lamp.'

'How we going to do that? We got to put them both out to pour the oil. You got any matches?'

Root felt through his pockets. 'Only two.'

'Now, you see? We got to hold this meeting with only one lamp. I should've looked things over this afternoon. I was busy in town, though. I thought I could leave it to you.'

'Maybe we could quick pour some of this oil in a can and then pour it into the other lamp.'

'Yeah, and then set the joint on fire. You're a hell of a helper.'

Root leaned back against the wall again. 'I wish they'd come. What time is it, Dick?'

'Five after eight.'

'Well, what's keeping them? What are they waiting for? Did you tell them eight o'clock?'

'Oh! Shut up, kid. You'll get my goat pretty soon. I don't know what's keeping them. Maybe they got cold feet. Now shut up for a little while.' He dug his hands into the pockets of his jacket again. 'Got a cigarette, Root?'

'No.'

It was very still. Nearer the centre of the town, automobiles were moving; the mutter of their engines and an occasional horn sounded. A dog barked unexcitedly at one of the houses nearby. The wind ruffled the locust trees in whishing gusts.

'Listen, Dick! Do you hear voices? I think they're coming.' They turned their heads and strained to listen.

'I don't hear nothing. You just thought you heard it.'

Root walked to one of the dirty windows and looked out. Coming back, he paused at the pile of pamphlets and straightened them neatly. 'What time is it now, Dick?'

'Keep still, will you? You'll drive me nuts. You got to have guts for this job. For God's sake show some guts.'

'Well, I never been out before, Dick.'

'Do you think anybody couldn't tell that? You sure make it plain enough.'

The wind gusted sharply in the locust trees. The front doors clicked and one of them opened slowly, squeaking a little at the hinges. The breeze came in, ruffled the pile of dusty newspapers in the corner and sailed the posters out from the wall like curtains.

'Shut that door, Root. . . . No, leave it open. Then we can hear them coming better.' He looked at his watch. 'It's nearly half past eight.'

'Do you think they'll come? How long we going to wait, if they don't show up?'

The older man stared at the open door. 'We ain't going to leave here before nine-thirty at the earliest. We got orders to hold this meeting.'

The night sounds came in more clearly through the open door—the dance of dry locust leaves on the road, the slow steady barking of the dog. On the wall the red and black portrait was menacing in the dim light. It floated out at the bottom again. Dick looked round at it. 'Listen, kid,' he said quietly. 'I know you're scared. When you're scared, just take a look at him.' He indicated the picture with his thumb. 'He wasn't scared. Just remember about what he did.'

The boy considered the portrait. 'You suppose he wasn't ever scared?'

Dick reprimanded him sharply. 'If he was, nobody ever found out about it. You take that for a lesson and don't go opening up for everybody to show them how you feel.'

'You're a good guy, Dick. I don't know what I'll do when I get sent out alone.'

'You'll be all right, kid. You got stuff in you. I can tell that. You just never been under fire.'

Root glanced quickly at the door. 'Listen! You hear somebody coming?'

'Lay off that stuff! When they get here, they'll get here.'

'Well—let's close the door. It's kind of cold in here. Listen! There *is* somebody coming.'

Quick footsteps sounded on the road, broke into a run and crossed the wooden sidewalk. A man in overalls and a painter's cap ran into the room. He was panting and winded. 'You guys better scram,' he said. 'There's a raiding party coming. None of the boys is coming to the meeting. They was going to let you take it, but I wouldn't do that. Come on! Get your stuff together and get out. That party's on the way.'

Root's face was pale and tight. He looked nervously at Dick. The older man shivered. He thrust his hands into his breast pockets and slumped his shoulders. 'Thanks,' he said. 'Thanks for telling us. You run along. We'll be all right.'

'The others was just going to leave you take it,' the man said.

Dick nodded. 'Sure, they can't see the future. They can't see beyond their nose. Run along now before you get caught.'

'Well, ain't you guys coming? I'll help carry some of your stuff.'

'We're going to stay,' Dick said woodenly. 'We got orders to stay. We got to take it.'

The man was moving towards the door. He turned back. 'Want me to stay with you?'

'No, you're a good guy. No need for you to stay. We could maybe use you some other time.'

'Well, I did what I could.'

III

Dick and Root heard him cross the wooden sidewalk and trot off into the darkness. The night resumed its sounds. The dead leaves scraped along the ground. The motors hummed from the centre of the town.

Root looked at Dick. He could see that the man's fists were doubled up in his breast pockets. The face muscles were stiff, but he smiled at the boy. The posters drifted out from the wall and settled back again.

'Scared, kid?'

Root bristled to deny it, and then gave it up. 'Yes, I'm scared. Maybe I won't be no good at this.'

'Take hold, kid!' Dick said fiercely. 'You take hold!'

Dick quoted to him, ' "The men of little spirit must have an example of stead—steadfastness. The people at large must have an example of injustice." There it is, Root. That's orders.' He relapsed into silence. The barking dog increased his tempo.

'I guess that's them,' said Root. 'Will they kill us, do you think?'

'No, they don't very often kill anybody.'

'But they'll hit us and kick us, won't they? They'll hit us in the face with sticks and break our nose. Big Mike, they broke his jaw in three places.'

'Take hold, kid! You take hold! And listen to me; if someone busts you, it isn't him that's doing it, it's the System. And it isn't you he's busting. He's taking a crack at the Principle. Can you remember that?'

'I don't want to run, Dick. Honest to God I don't. If I start to run, you hold me, will you?'

Dick walked near and touched him on the shoulder. 'You'll be all right. I can tell a guy that will stick.'

'Well, hadn't we better hide the lit'ature so it won't all get burned?'

'No—somebody might put a book in his pocket and read it later. Then it would be doing some good. Leave the books there. And shut up now! Talking only makes it worse.'

The dog had gone back to his slow, spiritless barking. A rush of wind brought a scurry of dead leaves in the open door. The portrait poster blew out and came loose at one corner. Root walked over and pinned it back. Somewhere in the town, an automobile squealed its brakes.

'Hear anything, Dick? Hear them coming yet?'

'No.'

'Listen, Dick. Big Mike lay two days with his jaw broke before anybody'd help him.'

The older man turned angrily on him. One doubled fist came out of his peajacket pocket. His eyes narrowed as he looked at the boy. He walked close and put an arm about his shoulders. 'Listen to me close, kid,' he said. 'I don't know much, but I been through this mill before. I can tell you this for sure. When it comes—it won't hurt. I don't know why, but it won't. Even if they kill you it won't hurt.' He dropped his arm and moved towards the front door. He looked out and listened in two directions before he came back into the room.

'Hear anything?'

'No. Not a thing.'

'What—do you think is keeping them?'

'How do you suppose I'd know?'

Root swallowed thickly. 'Maybe they won't come. Maybe it was all a lie that fella told us, just a joke.'

'Maybe.'

'Well, are—we going to wait all night to get our cans knocked off?'

Dick mimicked him. 'Yes, we're going to wait all night to get our cans knocked off.'

The wind sounded in one big fierce gust and then dropped away completely. The dog stopped barking. A train screamed for the crossing and went crashing by, leaving the night more silent than before. In a house nearby, an alarm clock went off. Dick said: 'Somebody goes to work early. Night watchman, maybe.' His voice was too loud in the stillness. The front door squeaked slowly shut.

'What time is it now, Dick?'

'Quarter past nine.'

'Jesus! Only that? I thought it was about morning. . . . Don't you wish they'd come and get it over, Dick? Listen, Dick!—I thought I heard voices.'

They stood stiffly, listening. Their heads were bent forward. 'You hear voices, Dick?'

'I think so. Like they're talking low.'

The dog barked again, fiercely this time. A little quiet murmur of voices could be heard. 'Look, Dick! I thought I saw somebody out the back window.'

The older man chuckled uneasily. 'That's so we can't get away. They got the place surrounded. Take hold, kid! They're coming now. Remember about it's not them, it's the System.'

There came a rushing clatter of footsteps. The doors burst open. A crowd of men thronged in, roughly dressed men, wearing black hats. They carried clubs and sticks in their hands. Dick and Root stood erect, their chins out, their eyes dropped and nearly closed.

Once inside, the raiders were uneasy. They stood in a half-circle about the two men, scowling, waiting for some one to move.

Young Root glanced sidewise at Dick and saw that the older man was looking at him coldly, critically, as though he judged his deportment. Root shoved his trembling hands in his pockets. He forced himself forward. His voice was shrill with fright. 'Comrades,' he shouted, 'you're just men like we are. We're all brothers——' A piece of two-by-four lashed out and struck him on the side of the head with a fleshy thump. Root went down to his knees and steadied himself with his hands.

The men stood still, glaring.

Root climbed slowly to his feet. His split ear spilled a red stream down his neck. The side of his face was mushy and purple. He got himself erect again. His breath burst passionately. His hands were steady now, his voice sure and strong. His eyes were hot with an ecstasy. 'Can't you see?' he shouted. 'It's all for you. We're doing it for you. All of it. You don't know what you're doing.'

'Kill the red rats!'

Someone giggled hysterically. And then the wave came. As he went down, Root caught a moment's glimpse of Dick's face smiling a tight, hard smile.

IV

He came near the surface several times, but didn't quite make it into consciousness. At last he opened his eyes and knew things. His face and head were heavy with bandages. He could only see a line of light between his puffed eyelids. For a time he lay, trying to think his way out. Then he heard Dick's voice near to him.

'You awake, kid?'

Root tried his voice and found that it croaked pretty badly. 'I guess so.'

'They sure worked out on your head. I thought you was gone. You was right about your nose. It ain't going to be very pretty.'

'What'd they do to you, Dick?'

'Oh, they bust my arm and a couple of ribs. You got to learn to turn your face down to the ground. That saves your eyes.' He paused and drew a careful breath. 'Hurts some to breathe when you get a rib bust. We are lucky. The cops picked us up and took us in.'

'Are we in jail, Dick?'

'Yeah! Hospital cell.'

'What they got on the book?'

He heard Dick try to chuckle, and gasp when it hurt him. 'Inciting to riot. We'll get six months, I guess. The cops got the lit'ature.'

'You won't tell them I'm under age, will you, Dick?'

'No. I won't. You better shut up. Your voice don't sound so hot. Take it easy.'

Root lay silent, muffled in a coat of dull pain. But in a moment he spoke again. 'It didn't hurt, Dick. It was funny. I felt all full up—and good.'

'You done fine, kid. You done as good as anybody I ever seen. I'll give you a blow to the committee. You just done fine.'

Root struggled to get something straight in his head. 'When they was busting me I wanted to tell them I didn't care.'

'Sure, kid. That's what I told you. It wasn't them. It was the System. You don't want to hate them. They don't know no better.'

Root spoke drowsily. The pain was muffling him under. 'You remember in the Bible, Dick, how it says something like "Forgive them because they don't know what they're doing"?'

Dick's reply was stern. 'You lay off that religion stuff, kid.' He quoted, ' "Religion is the opium of the people." '

'Sure, I know,' said Root. 'But there wasn't no religion to it. It was just—I felt like saying that. It was just kind of the way I felt.'

The Living

'How many dead people do you know?' said Mickser suddenly.

Immediately, painfully, I felt my answer would show me once more inferior to him. He was eight and I was a year younger. 'Do you mean ghosts? I said slowly, to gain time.

We were sitting one on each post of the big gate at the schoolhouse that was down on the main road.

'No,' said Mickser, 'I mean corpses.'

'But don't they get buried?' I cried.

'They're not buried for three days,' said Mickser scathingly. 'They have to be scrubbed and laid out and waked. You're not allowed to keep them any longer than that though, because their eyes go like this,' and he put his hands up to his eyes and drew down the lower lids to show the inner lids swimming with watery blood. 'They rot,' he explained.

'Mind would you fall!' said I hastily, thinking he might let go his eyelids if he had to steady himself on the gate-post.

We were sitting there watching the cars coming home from the Carlow and Kerry football finals. But it wasn't much fun. Cars were going past in plentiful numbers, all right, but spaced out fairly on the road, and moving nearly as slow as a funeral. As Mickser said, it was only the family man that came home straight after a match. The real followers didn't come home till night—or near morning, maybe.

'The sport is when the drunks are coming home,' Mickser said. 'Passing each other out on the roads—on the corners, mind! But your mammy wouldn't let a little fellow like you stay out long enough for that.'

It was only too true. It was a wonder she'd let me down to the road at all. She had a terrible dread of danger, my mammy. 'You can go down to the schoolhouse and look at the cars coming home if you're careful. And mind yourself!' she said to me. 'Keep well in from the road! And wait a minute. Don't sit up on that high wall, the way I saw you doing once.'

That was why we were up on the gate-posts, although they were much higher than the wall. 'Gate-posts isn't walls,' Mickser had said definitively.

That was Mickser all over. You could count on him to get you out of anything. But he could get you into anything, too. You never knew where a word would lead you with him. Still, this talk about dead people seemed safe enough.

'How many do you know, Mickser?' I asked, fearful but fascinated.

'Oh, I couldn't count them,' said Mickser loftily. 'I bet you don't know any at all.'

'My grandfather's dead.'

'How long is he dead?'

'He died the year I was born,' I said. 'On the very day after,' I added importantly, having heard it told by my mother to many people.

'Bah!' said Mickser. 'You can't count him. If you could, then you could count your great-grandfather, and your great-great-grandfather, and your great-great-great-grandfather, and . . .' He stopped enumerating them. 'Sure, isn't the ground full of dead people that nobody knew?' He pointed down below us to where, through the nettles, the clay under the wall showed black and sour. 'If you took up a spade this minute,' he said, 'and began digging down there, or anywhere, you'd be no time digging till you'd come on bones; somebody's bones! Oh, no!' He shook his head. 'You can't count people you didn't *see* dead, like my Uncle Bat that was sitting up eating a boiled egg one minute and lying back dead the next minute. He's the best one on my list, though,' he added magnanimously. 'I saw him alive *and* dead. But most of them I only saw dead—like my two aunts that died within a week of each other. Everyone said it was a pity, if they had to go, it couldn't have been closer together, so they could have made the one wake of it. How many is that?' he asked. 'How many have I now?'

'Only three,' I said, and my heart rose. He mightn't be able to think of any more.

He looked at me severely. He was a bit of a mind reader, as well as everything else. 'I wanted to pick out the good ones for first,' he said.

That overwhelmed me altogether. 'Ah, sure, Mickser,' I said. 'You needn't strain yourself thinking of good ones for one, because I never saw one at all. One of my aunts died a year ago, all right, and they had to take me to the funeral because they had no one to leave me with, but they wouldn't let me into the house till the funeral was ready to move off. They took it in turns to sit out in the car with me.'

'And what was that for?' said Mickser, looking blankly at me.

'I don't know,' I said in a grieved voice, but after a bit, in fairness to my mother and father, I felt obliged to hazard a reason for their behaviour. 'Maybe they thought I'd dream about it.'

This seemed to give Mickser cause for profound reflection. We sat saying nothing for a long time. I was thinking back over it myself. 'Not that it did much good keeping me outside,' I said. 'Because I dreamt about it all the same. I kept them up till morning, nightmaring about coffins and hearses!'

'Coffins and hearses?' Mickser repeated. 'What was there about them to have you nightmaring? It's corpses that give people the creeps.' He looked at me with genuine interest. 'I wonder what way you'd take on if you saw a corpse,' he said. And then he snapped his fingers. 'I have it!' he said. 'There's a wake in a cottage the other side of the town.'

'Mind would you fall!' I cried—urgently this time, because of the way he was hopping about on his pants with excitement.

'Do you know the cottage I mean? It's at the level-crossing. Do you know the woman in it—the one that opens and shuts the railway gates? Well, her man is dead.'

'A big fellow with red hair, is it?'

'That's the one!' he cried. 'She used to have him sitting outside the cottage most days, on a chair in the sun. He was a class of delicate ever since he was hit by the train.' Deftly Mickser tapped his own pate. 'Up here,' he said. 'He died this morning. Isn't it a bit of luck I was put in mind of it? But we'd want to get there quick,' he said, taking one jump down off the gate-post, into the nettles and all, without minding them any more than if he was a dog. 'Before the crowds,' he said. 'They'll be glad to see us no matter who we are if we're the first to come. They're always glad to see the first signs of people arriving after the cleaning and work they've been doing. And they love to see children above all—at first, that is to say. "Look who we have here," they say,' he mimicked in a voice that nearly made myself fall off the post. ' "Bless their little hearts," ' he went on. ' "Come in, child," they say and they lead you inside, telling each other that there's no prayers like the prayers of a child. Up they bring you straight to the bed, and down they put you kneeling beside it where you can get a good gawk at everything. Oh, but it's a different story altogether, I can tell you, if you leave it till late in the evening. You haven't a chance of getting inside the door. "Out of this with you, you little brats!" That's all you'd hear then. "This is no place for children—out of it now!" They'd take the yard brush to you if you didn't get yourself out of sight double quick. So we'd better get up there immediately,' he said. 'What are you waiting for?'

I was hanging back for more reasons than one. 'I was told to stay here,' I said.

'You were told not to be climbing, too,' said Mickser, as quick as a lawyer. 'So you can't say you were doing what you were told, anyway—not but that it's doing all you're told that has you the way you are this day, knowing nothing about anything. To think they wouldn't let you see your own aunt laid out! I know it wouldn't be me that would be done out of a thing like that. And, what's more, you oughtn't to put up with it, either. You ought to tell them there'd be no nightmaring or carrying on about corpses if you were let get used to them like me. Are you coming, or are you not?'

It was a sweet, mild afternoon as we set out for the edge of the town to where the level-crossing was, and the small slate-roofed house to one side of it. It was very familiar to me when I was a bit smaller and my mother used to take me for a walk out of town into the country air. We often had to wait for the gates to be opened for us, although the train would have thundered past.

'What is the delay?' my mother would ask impatiently.

'I have to wait for the signals, ma'am,' the woman in charge of the gates would say. 'You can pass through the wicket gate if you like, ma'am, but that's none of my responsibility.'

'Oh, we're not in a hurry,' my mother would say hastily, doubtless to give me a good example of caution.

But there was no need. I had heard Mickser say he put a halfpenny on the line one day and the train made a penny out of it. I had no fancy for being flattened out to the size of a man. And, anyway, I used to be very curious about the big white-faced man that would always be sitting in the little bit of garden on a chair—a chair brought out of the house, not one you'd leave outside, like we had in the garden at home.

'Do they take it in at night?' I asked once.

'Of course she does,' said my mother in a shocked voice, but she must have thought I meant the man. 'Please don't stare,' she'd say to me. 'Why do I have to keep telling you!'

Only when the gates were opened, and we were starting to cross over the rails, would she let on to see him for her part. It was always the same. 'How is he today?' she'd ask the woman.

And the woman's answer was always the same, too. 'Poorly.' That's what she'd say. At times, though rarely, she'd add: 'It's a great cross to me, but I suppose God knows what He's doing.'

'We must hope so anyway,' my mother would say to that, and she'd step over the rails more quickly, till we were on the other side. 'How is it,' she said testily to me when we were out of earshot, 'those gates are always shut no matter what time of the day we want to pass?'

And now here, today, for the first time in my life, the railway gates were wide open.

'Do you think they might have forgot to close them, on account of the wake?' I said, hanging back nervously.

Mickser stood in the middle of the tracks and looked back at me. 'God knows it's high time someone took you in hand,' he said. 'You're nothing but an old babby. What harm would it be if they did forget? Haven't you eyes? Haven't you ears? And, if it comes to that, haven't you legs? Come on out of that!' But he slowed down himself, and looked up and down the line.

*

'We're the first here,' he said when we got to the cottage. He sized up the look of the little house expertly. 'They're not finished yet,' he said.

To me the house looked as if it had been washed down from top to bottom, the way I was washed down myself every Sunday night, and the bit of garden outside it was the same, neatened and tidied, and the big stones that I used to remark around the flower-beds, keeping back the clay from the grass, were whitewashed, every one of them. It was a treat—the stones bright white, and the clay bright black, with not one weed to be seen out of all the weeds there used to be everywhere. But the chair wasn't out.

'We're too early,' Mickser said, and he stepped suddenly over to the window that was to one side of the door, me at his heels. Being behind him, I couldn't see near so well but I saw enough to open my mouth. Between white counter-panes and white tablecloths and white mantle cloths and white doilies, the place was got up like the chapel at Lady Day. And in the middle of it all, like the high altar, was a big bed with a counterpane as white and glossy as marble, and . . .

But Mickser didn't let me see any more. He pulled me away. 'I don't think they're ready yet,' he said. He seemed to be losing courage just as I was getting mine. He put his hands in his pockets and sauntered towards the door. 'There now, what did I tell you!' he cried, as we only missed getting drenched to the skin by a big basin of slops that was sloshed out the door at that minute.

'Did you ever walk the railroad tracks?' he asked suddenly. And I knew he'd let up altogether on going to the wake.

'I'm not allowed to walk on the tracks,' I said. Anyway, I was bent on seeing the bed better, and what was on it. 'Let me get a look in the window, at least,' I said, and I skipped over the flowers and pasted my face to the glass.

What did I expect to see? I don't know. Not the great grey man that was carved out on the bed, hard as stone, all but his red hair; that was real-looking, like the hair on a doll. 'Eh, Mickser. Could you give me a leg-up on the window-sill?' I cried, getting more and more curious and excited.

'Are you pots?' said Mickser. 'If they came out and caught you up on that window-sill you'd be clouted out of here with one of those stones.'

'A true word if ever there was one!' said a voice at that moment, and a thin bit of a woman in black came round the gable-end with her sleeves rolled up and no smile on her, I can tell you. 'Out of here with you!' she shouted. 'This is no place for you!' Just the very thing Mickser said wouldn't be said to us.

But before we had time to get out of the flower-bed another woman came running out of the front door—the woman herself that used to have charge of the crossing gates. 'It's not right to send anyone from the door of a dead-house,' she said dully.

'Hush now, they're only gossoons,' said the other one.

'He was only a gossoon, too, in the latter end,' said our woman. 'Only a child—that was what the priest said to me many a time. Not that I had much chance of knowing what a real child is like! Sure, we were no length married when he was struck by the train. I never thought on our wedding day that he'd be all the babby I'd ever have!'

'There now! There now!' said the other one. 'Isn't it better God took him before yourself, anyway?'

'I used to pray He would,' said the woman. 'But now I'm not so sure. Wasn't it the unnatural thing to have to pray for, anyway? Doesn't every woman pray for the opposite— to die before them and not be left a lonesome widda-woman? Ah, wasn't it a hard thing to be one year praying God to send you a man, and the next praying to have him taken? Oh, it's little you know about it.'

She was getting a bit wild-looking, and the other woman began dragging at her to get her back into the house. 'Hush now, you'll feel different when time goes on.'

'Will I?' said the woman, looking wonderingly at the other one. 'I'll feel different, maybe, sometimes when I look at the clock and have to pull off my apron and run out to throw back the gates. I'll feel different, maybe, when some woman stops to have a word with me, or when I have to take the jug and go down the road for a cup of milk. But in the middle of the night, or first thing when the jackdaws start screaming in the chimney and wake me out of my sleep, will I feel different then? And what if I do forget?' she cried, suddenly pulling her arm free. 'I'll have nothing at all then! It will be like as if I never had him at all.' She put her hand up to her head at that and began brushing her hair back from her forehead.

Stepping behind her back, the woman that wanted to be rid of us signalled at us to make off with ourselves, but it was too late. The dead man's wife started forward and caught us by the hands. 'We must make the most of every minute we have him!' she cried. 'Come inside and see him.' She pushed us in the doorway.

'Kneel down and say a prayer for him,' she commanded, pushing us down on our knees, but her voice was wonderfully gentle now where it had been wild. 'It's many a day since he was able to pray for himself,' she said softly. 'I used to long for him to be able to say one little prayer, and I was always trying to bring them to his mind, but he couldn't recall a word of them. When he'd be sitting out in the sun

on his chair I used to show him the flowers and remind him
God made them. And do you know all he'd say?' She gave
a little laugh before she told us. ' "Who's that fellow?"
he'd say. And he'd look round to see if He was behind
him! But the priest said God wouldn't heed him; he said
He'd make allowances for him.'

I was half listening. When she had us kneel down I put
my hands up to my face and I started to say my prayers,
but after a minute or two I opened my fingers and took a
look out through them at the man on the bed. Why was
she saying he was like a child? He was a man if ever I saw
one! Just then the woman swooped down on me. She saw
me looking at him. I thought she might be mad with me,
but it was the opposite.

'If only he could see you here now beside him,' she said.
She leaned across me and began to stroke his hands. 'Here's
two nice little boys come to see you!' she said, and then her
eyes got very bright and wild again. 'He never had a soul
come into the house to see him in twenty years. He never
had another human being but one as much as put out a
hand to touch him—isn't that a lonely thing to think? Him
that was so friendly before his accident that he knew every
man on the whole line, even to the engine-drivers and
stokers. He knew them all by their names. And as for the
passengers! Do you know what? Look out at that garden.
Every twig in it was grown from a shoot or a cutting thrown
out to him in a paper parcel by somebody that got to know
him shuttling back and forth past the gates! Oh, there never
was such a man for making friends! And to think it's twenty
years since anyone shook him by the hand. Oh, isn't it a
queer world?'

It was indeed, I thought. I wonder would it be any use me shaking hands with him now, I thought, and it might be she saw the thought in my eyes.

'Would it be asking too much of you to stroke his hand?' she said, and then, as if she had settled it in her own mind that it wouldn't be asking much at all, she got very excited. 'Stand up, like good boys,' she said, 'and stroke his hands. No, wait a minute!' she cried, and she got another idea, and she delved her hand into her pocket. 'How would you like to comb his hair?' she cried.

I was nearer to the head of the bed than Mickser, but Mickser was nearer to her than me, and I couldn't be sure which of us she meant. I wanted above all to be polite, and I stood up, so as to be ready in case it was me she meant. She was taking a few big red hairs off the comb. Mickser stood up, too, but it was only to give me a shove out of his way.

'Let me out of here!' he shouted, and, putting the woman and me to either side of him, he bolted for the door. The next minute he was flying across the tracks.

*

And me after him. I told you I wanted to be polite to the people, the dead one included, but after all it was Mickser brought me, and it wouldn't be very polite to him to stay on after him. Not that he showed any appreciation.

I was full of talk. 'Well! I have one for my list, anyway, now,' I said cheerfully.

'I suppose you have,' he said—kind of grudgingly, I thought—and then he nearly spoiled it all on me. 'That one oughtn't to count, by rights,' he said. 'He wasn't all in it when he was alive; he was sort of dead all along.' He tapped his pate again, as he did the first time. 'Up here!' he added.

I thought about that for a minute. 'He looked all in it there on the bed!' I said.

But Mickser didn't seem to take well to talking about him at all. 'Come on back to the main road,' he said. 'The cars are coming along now. Can't you hear them? Some of those boyos have a few jars in them, I'd say, in spite of the wives. Come on!'

'Ah, you can go and watch them yourself,' I said. 'I'm going home.'

The truth was I was too excited to sit on any wall for long. I wanted to go home because there were a few things I'd like to find out from Mother, if I could bring the talk around to the topic of corpses without letting on where I got the information I had already.

As I ran off from Mickser across the fields for home, I felt that I was a new man, and I felt sure they would all notice a change in me when I went into the house. The next time there was a funeral there would be no need to leave me sitting out in a car.

'Wipe your feet, son!' my mother cried out to me through the open door of the kitchen the minute I came in sight. 'Not that you'd be the only one to put tracks all over the place,' she said, and I could see what she meant, because there in the middle of the floor was my brother's old bike, up-ended, with the wheels in the air, and he busy mending a puncture. Or was it my father she meant? Because he was sitting the other side of the fire, with his feet in a basin of water.

It must have been my father she meant, because she lit on him just then. 'This is no place for washing your feet,' she said. 'There's a fire inside in the parlour. Why don't you go in there and wash them? I haven't got room to turn around with you all.'

'The parlour is no place for washing feet,' said my father quietly, and he pointed to the bike in the middle of the floor. 'When that fellow's done with that bike you'll be glad to have a bit of water on the floor to swish out the mess he'll have made. Why don't you make him take it out in the yard?'

My mother sighed. She was always sighing, but they weren't the kind of sighs you'd heed. They were caused by something we'd done on her, but they were sighs of patience, if you know what I mean, and not complaint.

'It's a bit cold outside,' she said. 'Here, you, son,' she said, turning to me. She picked up my satchel and shoved it under my arm. 'Let you set a good example and go into the parlour and do your home-work there by the nice fire.'

But I wasn't going into the empty parlour.

'Dear *knows*! I don't know why I waste my time lighting that fire every day and none of you ever set foot in there until it's nearly night. I only wish I could go in and sit by it. Then I'd leave you the kitchen and welcome.'

But I think she knew well that if she was to go in there that minute it wouldn't be many minutes more till we'd all be in there along with her, myself and my satchel, and my father with his feet in the basin, and the old bike as well, if it could be squeezed in at all between the piano and the chiffonier and all the other big, useless pieces of furniture that were kept in there out of the way.

'Ah, sure, aren't we all right here,' said my father. 'Where we can be looking at you?'

'You must have very little worth looking at if you want to be looking at me,' said my mother, in a sort of voice I knew well; it sounded cross but couldn't be, because she always stretched up when she spoke like that, so she'd see into the little mirror on the mantelshelf, and she always smiled at what she saw in the glass. And well she might. She was a pretty woman, my mother, and never more so than when we were all around her in the kitchen, annoying her and making her cheeks red with the fuss of keeping us in order.

'Mind would you catch your finger in the spokes of that wheel!' she cried just then to my brother.

'Mind would you catch your hair in it, my girl,' said Father, because as the kettle boiled and the little kitchen got full of steam, her hair used to loosen and lop round her face like a girl's. And he caught ahold of her as if to pull her back from the bike.

'Let go of me!' she cried. 'Will you never get sense?'

'I hope not,' said my father. 'And, what is more, I don't want you to get too much of it, either,' he said.

'Oh, go on with you and your old talk, before the boys and all!' she cried, and she tried to drag herself free.

'She's not as strong as her tongue would have us believe, boys,' said my father, tightening his hold. And then he laughed. 'You'll never be the man I am!' he said, and this time it was my mother herself that giggled.

That very minute, in the middle of tricking and laughing, my father's face changed, and it was as if he wasn't holding her for fun at all but the way he'd hold us if he had something against us.

'You're feeling all right these days, aren't you?' he cried. 'You'd tell me if you weren't, wouldn't you?' And then he let her go and put his hands up to his head. 'Oh, my God, what would I do if anything happened to you!' he said.

'Such talk!' said my mother again, but her voice sounded different, too. And although she was free, she didn't ask to move away but stood there beside him, with such a sad look on her face I wanted to cry.

And I knew I couldn't pester her with questions about the poor fellow at the level-crossing. But I thought about him. And I thought of the words of the prayers we said every night, '. . . the living and the dead . . .' Over and over we'd said them, night after night, and I never had paid any heed. But I suddenly felt that they were terrible, terrible words, and if we were to be kneeling down at that moment saying them, I couldn't bear it; I'd start nightmaring there and then, in the middle of them all, with the lamps lit, and it not dark.

The kettle began to spit on the range, and my mother ran over and lifted it back from the blaze. 'How about us taking our tea in the parlour?' she cried. 'All of us. The kitchen is no fitter than the backyard with you!'

And in the excitement I forgot all about the living and the dead. For a long time.

ALAN SILLITOE

Uncle Ernest

A MIDDLE-AGED man wearing a dirty raincoat, who badly needed a shave and looked as though he hadn't washed for a month, came out of a public lavatory with a cloth bag of tools folded beneath his arm. Standing for a moment on the edge of the pavement to adjust his cap—the cleanest thing about him—he looked casually to left and right and, when the flow of traffic had eased off, crossed the road. His name and trade were always spoken in one breath, even when the nature of his trade was not in question: Ernest Brown the upholsterer. Every night before returning to his lodgings he left the bag of tools for safety with a man who looked after the public lavatory near the town centre, for he felt there was a risk of them being lost or stolen should he take them back to his room, and if such a thing were to happen his living would be gone.

Chimes to the value of half past ten boomed from the Council-house clock. Over the theatre patches of blue sky held hard-won positions against autumnal clouds, and a treacherous wind lashed out its gusts, sending paper and cigarette packets cartwheeling along unswept gutters. Empty-bellied Ernest was ready for his breakfast, so walked through a café doorway, instinctively lowering his head as he did so, though the beams were a foot above his height.

The long spacious eating-place was almost full. Ernest usually arrived for his breakfast at nine o'clock, but having been paid ten pounds for re-covering a three-piece in a public house the day before, he had stationed himself in the Saloon Bar for the rest of the evening to drink jar after jar of beer, in a slow, prolonged and concentrated way that lonely men have. As a result it had been difficult to drag himself from drugged and blissful sleep this morning. His face was pale and his eyes an unhealthy yellow: when he spoke only a few solitary teeth showed behind his lips.

Having passed through the half-dozen noisy people standing about he found himself at the counter, a scarred and chipped haven for hands, like a littered invasion beach extending between two headlands of tea urns. The big fleshy brunette was busy, so he hastily scanned the list written out in large white letters on the wall behind. He made a timid gesture with his hand. 'A cup of tea, please.'

The brunette turned on him. Tea swilled from a huge brown spout—into a cup that had a crack emerging like a hair above the layer of milk—and a spoon clinked after it into the stream. 'Anything else?'

He spoke up hesitantly. 'Tomatoes on toast as well.' Picking up the plate pushed over to him he moved slowly backwards out of the crowd, then turned and walked towards a vacant corner table.

A steamy appetizing smell rose from the plate: he took up the knife and fork and, with the sharp clean action of a craftsman, cut off a corner of the toast and tomato and raised it slowly to his mouth, eating with relish and hardly noticing people sitting roundabout. Each wielding of his knife and fork, each geometrical cut of the slice of toast, each curve and twist of his lips joined in a complex and regular motion that gave him great satisfaction. He ate slowly, quietly and contentedly, aware only of himself and his body being warmed and made tolerable once more by food. The leisurely movement of spoon and cup and saucer made up the familiar noise of late breakfast in a crowded café, sounded like music flowing here and there in variations of rhythm.

For years he had eaten alone, but was not yet accustomed to loneliness. He could not get used to it, had only adapted himself to it temporarily in the hope that one day its spell would break. Ernest remembered little of his past, and life moved under him so that he hardly noticed its progress. There was no strong memory to entice him to what had gone by, except that of dead and dying men straggling barbed wire between the trenches in the first world war. Two sentences had dominated his lips during the years that followed: 'I should not be here in England. I should be dead with the rest of them in France.' Time bereft him of these sentences, till only a dull wordless image remained.

People, he found, treated him as if he were a ghost, as if he were not made of flesh and blood—or so it seemed— and from then on he had lived alone. His wife left him—due to his too vile temper, it was said—and his brothers went to other towns. Later he had thought to look them up, but decided against it: for even in this isolation only the will to go forward and accept more of it seemed worth while. He felt in a dim indefinite way that to go back and search out the slums and landmarks of his youth, old friends, the smells and sounds that beckoned him tangibly from better days, was a sort of death. He argued that it was best to leave them alone, because it seemed somehow probable that after death—whenever it came—he would meet all these things once again.

No pink scar marked his flesh from shellshock and a jolted brain, and so what had happened in the war warranted no pension book, and even to him the word 'injury' never came into his mind. It was just that he did not care any more: the wheel of the years had broken him, and so had made life tolerable. When the next war came his back was not burdened at first, and even the fines and days in prison that he was made to pay for being without Identity Card or Ration Book—or for giving them away with a glad heart to deserters—did not lift him from his tolerable brokenness. The nightmare hours of gunfire and exploding bombs revived a dull image long suppressed as he stared blankly at the cellar wall of his boarding house, and even threw into his mind the scattered words of two insane sentences. But, considering the time-scale his life was lived on, the war ended quickly, and again nothing mattered. He lived from hand to mouth, working cleverly at settees and sofas and chairs, caring about no one. When work was difficult to find and life was hard, he did not notice it very much, and now that he was prosperous and had enough money, he also detected little difference, spending what he earned on beer, and never once thinking that he needed a new coat or a solid pair of boots.

He lifted the last piece of toast and tomato from his plate, then felt dregs of tea moving against his teeth. When he had finished chewing he lit a cigarette and was once more aware of people sitting around him. It was eleven o'clock and the low-roofed café was slowly emptying, leaving only a dozen people inside. He knew that at one table they were talking about horse-racing and at another about war, but words only flowed into his ears and entered his mind at a low pitch of comprehension, leaving it calm and content as he vaguely contemplated the positions and patterns of tables about the room. There would be no work until two o'clock, so he intended sitting where he was until then. Yet a sudden embarrassment at having no food on the table to justify a prolonged occupation of it sent him to the counter for tea and cakes.

As he was being served two small girls came in. One sat at a table but the second and elder stood at the counter. When he returned to his place he found the younger girl sitting there. He was confused and shy, but nevertheless sat down to drink tea and cut a cake into four pieces. The girl looked at him and continued to do so until the elder one came from the counter carrying two cups of steaming tea.

They sat talking and drinking, utterly oblivious of Ernest, who slowly felt their secretive, childish animation enter into himself. He glanced at them from time to time, feeling as if he should not be there, though when he looked at them he did so in a gentle way, with kind, full-smiling eyes. The elder girl, about twelve years old, was dressed in a brown coat that was too big for her, and though she was talking and laughing most of the time he noticed the paleness of her face and her large round eyes that he would have thought beautiful had he not detected the familiar type of vivacity that expressed neglect and want.

The smaller girl was less lively and merely smiled as she answered her sister with brief curt words. She drank her tea and warmed her hands at the same time without putting the cup down once until she had emptied it. Her thin red fingers curled round the cup as she stared into the leaves, and gradually the talk between them died down and they were silent, leaving the field free for traffic that could be heard moving along the street outside, and for inside noises made by the brunette who washed cups and dishes ready for the rush that was expected at mid-day dinner-time.

Ernest was calculating how many yards of rexine would be needed to cover the job he was to do that afternoon, but when the younger girl began speaking he listened to her, hardly aware that he was doing so.

'If you've got any money I'd like a cake, our Alma.'

'I haven't got any more money,' the elder one replied impatiently.

'Yes you have, and I'd like a cake.'

She was adamant, almost aggressive. 'Then you'll have to want on, because I've only got tuppence.'

'You can buy a cake with that,' the young girl persisted, twining her fingers round the empty cup. 'We don't need bus fares home because it ain't far to walk.'

'We can't walk home: it might rain.'

'No it won't.'

'Well *I* want a cake as well, but I'm not walking all that way,' the elder girl said conclusively, blocking any last gap that might remain in her defences. The younger girl gave up and said nothing, looked emptily in front of her.

Ernest had finished eating and took out a cigarette, struck a match across the iron fastening of a table leg and, having inhaled deeply, allowed smoke to wander from his mouth. Like a gentle tide washing in under the moon, a line of water flowing inwards and covering the sand, a feeling of acute loneliness took hold of him, an agony that would not let him weep. The two girls sat before him wholly engrossed in themselves, still debating whether they should buy a cake or whether they should ride home on a bus.

'But it'll be cold,' reasoned the elder, 'walking home.'

'No it won't,' the other said, but with no conviction in her words. The sound of their voices told him how lonely he was, each word feeding him with so much more loneliness that he felt utterly unhappy and empty.

Time went slowly: the minute-hand of the clock seemed as if it were nailed immovably at one angle. The two girls looked at each other and did not notice him: he withdrew into himself and felt the emptiness of the world and wondered how he would spend all the days that seemed to stretch vacantly, like goods on a broken-down conveyor belt, before him. He tried to remember things that had happened and felt panic when he discovered a thirty-year vacuum. All he could see behind was a grey mist and all he could see before him was the same unpredictable fog that would hide nothing. He wanted to walk out of the café and find some activity so that he would henceforth be able to mark off the passage of his empty days, but he had no will to move. He heard someone crying so shook himself free of such thoughts and saw the younger girl with hands to her eyes, weeping. 'What's the matter?' he asked tenderly, leaning across the table.

The elder girl replied for her, saying sternly:

'Nothing. She's acting daft.'

'But she must be crying for some reason. What is it?' Ernest persisted, quietly and soothingly, bending closer still towards her. 'Tell me what's wrong.' Then he remembered something. He drew it like a live thread from a mixture of reality and dream, hanging on to vague words that floated back into his mind. The girl's conversation came to him through an intricate process of recollection. 'I'll get you something to eat,' he ventured. 'Can I?'

She unscrewed clenched fingers from her eyes and looked up, while the elder girl glared at him resentfully and said: 'We don't want anything. We're going now.'

'No, don't go,' he cried. 'You just sit down and see what I'm going to get for you.' He stood up and walked to the counter, leaving them whispering to each other.

He came back with a plate of pastries and two cups of tea, which he set before the girls, who looked on in silence. The younger was smiling now. Her round eager eyes were fascinated, yet followed each movement of his hands with some apprehension. Though still hostile the elder girl was gradually subdued by the confidently working actions of his hands, by caressing words and the kindness that showed in his face. He was wholly absorbed in doing good and, at the same time, fighting the feeling of loneliness that he still remembered, but only as a nightmare is remembered.

The two children fell under his spell, began to eat cakes and sip the tea. They glanced at each other, and then at Ernest as he sat before them smoking a cigarette. The café was still almost empty, and the few people eating were so absorbed in themselves, or were in so much of a hurry to eat their food and get out that they took little notice of the small company in the corner. Now that the atmosphere between himself and the two girls had grown more friendly Ernest began to talk to them. 'Do you go to school?' he asked.

The elder girl automatically assumed control and

answered his questions. 'Yes, but today we had to come down town on an errand for our mam.'

'Does your mother go out to work, then?'

'Yes,' she informed him. 'All day.'

Ernest was encouraged. 'And does she cook your dinners?'

She obliged him with another answer. 'Not until night.'

'What about your father?' he went on.

'He's dead,' said the smaller girl, her mouth filled with food, daring to speak outright for the first time. Her sister looked at her with disapproval, making it plain that she had said the wrong thing and that she should only speak under guidance.

'Are you going to school then this afternoon?' Ernest resumed.

'Yes,' the spokesman said.

He smiled at her continued hard control. 'And what's your name then?'

'Alma,' she told him, 'and hers is Joan.' She indicated the smaller girl with a slight nod of the head.

'Are you often hungry?'

She stopped eating and glanced at him, uncertain how to answer. 'No, not much,' she told him non-committally, busily eating a second pastry.

'But you were today?'

'Yes,' she said, casting away diplomacy like the crumpled cake paper she let fall to the floor.

He said nothing for a few moments, sitting with knuckles pressed to his lips. 'Well, look'—he began suddenly talking again—'I come in here every day for my dinner, just about half past twelve, and if ever you're feeling hungry, come down and see me.'

They agreed to this, accepted sixpence for their bus fares home, thanked him very much, and said goodbye.

*

During the following weeks they came to see him almost every day. Sometimes, when he had little money, he filled his empty stomach with a cup of tea while Alma and Joan satisfied themselves on five shillings'-worth of more solid food. But he was happy and gained immense satisfaction from seeing them bending hungrily over eggs, bacon, and pastries, and he was so smoothed at last into a fine feeling of having something to live for that he hardly remembered the lonely days when his only hope of being able to talk to someone was by going into a public house to get drunk. He was happy now because he had his 'little girls' to look after, as he came to call them.

He began spending all his money to buy them presents, so that he was often in debt at his lodgings. He still did not buy any clothes, for whereas in the past his money had been swilled away on beer, now it was spent on presents and food for the girls, and he went on wearing the same old dirty mackintosh and was still without a collar to his shirt; even his cap was no longer clean.

Every day, straight out of school, Alma and Joan ran to catch a bus for the town centre and, a few minutes later, smiling and out of breath, walked into the café where Ernest was waiting. As days and weeks passed, and as Alma noticed how much Ernest depended on them for company, how happy he was to see them, and how obviously miserable when they did not come for a day—which was rare now—she began to demand more and more presents, more food, more money, but only in a particularly naïve and childish way, so that Ernest, in his oblivious contentment, did not notice it.

But certain customers of the café who came in every day could not help but see how the girls asked him to buy them this and that, and how he always gave in with a nature too good to be decently true, and without the least sign of realizing what was really happening. He would never dream to question their demands, for to him these two girls whom he looked upon almost as his own daughters were the only people he had to love.

★

Ernest, about to begin eating, noticed two smartly dressed men sitting at a table a few yards away. They had sat in the same place the previous day, and also the day before that, but he thought no more about it because Joan and Alma came in and walked quickly across to his table.

'Hello, Uncle Ernest!' they said brightly. 'What can we have for dinner?' Alma looked across at the chalk-written list on the wall to read what dishes were available.

His face changed from the blank preoccupation of eating, and a smile of happiness infused his cheeks, eyes, and the curve of his lips. 'Whatever you like,' he answered.

'But what have they got?' Alma demanded crossly. 'I can't read their scrawl.'

'Go up to the counter and ask for a dinner,' he advised with a laugh.

'Will you give me some money then?' she asked, her

hand out. Joan stood by without speaking, lacking Alma's confidence, her face timid, and nervous because she did not yet understand this regular transaction of money between Ernest and themselves, being afraid that one day they would stand there waiting for money and Ernest would quite naturally look surprised and say there was nothing for them.

He had just finished repairing an antique three-piece and had been paid that morning, so Alma took five shillings and they went to the counter for a meal. While they were waiting to be served the two well-dressed men who had been watching Ernest for the last few days stood up and walked over to him.

Only one of them spoke; the other held his silence and looked on. 'Are those two girls your daughters, or any relation to you?' the first asked, nodding towards the counter.

Ernest looked up and smiled. 'No,' he explained in a mild voice, 'they're just friends of mine, why?'

The man's eyes were hard, and he spoke clearly. 'What kind of friends?'

'Just friends. Why? Who are you?' he shuddered, feeling a kind of half guilt growing inside him for a half-imagined reason that he hoped wasn't true

'Never mind who we are. I just want you to answer my question.'

Ernest raised his voice slightly, yet did not dare to look into the man's arrogant eyes. 'Why?' he cried. 'What's it got to do with you? Why are you asking questions like this?'

'We're from the police station,' the man remarked dryly, 'and we've had complaints that you're giving these little girls money and leading them the wrong way!'

Ernest wanted to laugh, but only from misery. Yet he did

not want to laugh in case he should annoy the two detectives. He started to talk: 'But . . . but . . .'—then found himself unable to go on. There was much that he wanted to say, yet he could enunciate nothing, and a bewildered animal stare moved slowly into his eyes.

'Look,' the man said emphatically, 'we don't want any of your "buts". We know all about you. We know who you are. We've known you for years in fact, and we're asking you to leave those girls alone and have nothing more to do with them. Men like you shouldn't be giving money to little girls. You should know what you're doing, and have more sense.'

Ernest protested loudly at last. 'I tell you they're friends of mine. I mean no harm. I look after them and give them presents just as I would daughters of my own. They're the only company I've got. In any case why shouldn't I look after them? Why should you take them away from me? Who do you think you are? Leave me alone . . . leave me alone.' His voice had risen to a weak scream of defiance, and the other people in the crowded café were looking around and staring at him wondering what was the cause of the disturbance.

The two detectives acted quickly and competently, yet without apparent haste. One stood on each side of him, lifted him up, and walked him by the counter, out on to the street, squeezing his wrists tightly as they did so. As Ernest passed the counter he saw the girls holding their plates, looking in fear and wonder at him being walked out.

They took him to the end of the street, and stood there for a few seconds talking to him, still keeping hold of his wrists and pressing their fingers hard into them.

'Now look here, we don't want any more trouble from *you*, but if ever we see you near those girls again you'll find yourself up before a magistrate.' The tone of finality in his voice possessed a physical force that pushed Ernest to the brink of sanity.

He stood speechless. He wanted to say so many things, but the words would not come to his lips. They quivered helplessly with shame and hatred, and so were incapable of making words. 'We're asking you in a peaceful manner,' the detective went on, 'to leave them alone. Understand?'

'Yes,' Ernest was forced to answer.

'Right. Go on then. And we don't want to see you with those girls again.'

He was only aware of the earth sliding away from under his feet, and a wave of panic crashing into his mind, and he felt the unbearable and familiar emptiness that flowed outwards from a tiny and unknowable point inside him. Then he was filled with hatred for everything, then intense pity for all the movement that was going on around him, and finally even more intense pity for himself. He wanted to cry but could not: he could only walk away from his shame.

Then he began to shed agony at each step. His bitterness eddied away and a feeling the depth of which he had never known before took its place. There was now more purpose in the motion of his footsteps as he went along the pavement through mid-day crowds. And it seemed to him that he did not care about anything any more as he pushed through the swing doors and walked into the crowded and noisy bar of a public house, his stare fixed by a beautiful heavily baited trap of beer pots that would take him into the one and only best kind of oblivion.

BILL NAUGHTON

Late Night on Watling Street

———— ✦ ————

IT WAS after midnight when I drew my lorry on to the parking ground in front of 'Lew's' caff. I switched off the engine and lights, got out of the cab, knew it would be safe without locking it up, and stretched my limbs and looked up at the sky. It was all starry. The air had a nice fresh rinsed taste to it. I walked round the wagon and kicked my tyres, testing the ropes round my load, and with that nice week-end feeling you get on a Friday night, I went inside.

It was nearly empty. I went up to the counter. Ethel, Lew's young wife, was making a fresh pot of tea, and Lew was watching her. I heard him say, 'Make it any stronger an' you'll hatta serve it with knives and forks.'

'I can't stand the sight of weak tea,' said Ethel.

'You can get it a good colour without putting all that much in,' said Lew.

'It's not the colour a man wants,' said Ethel, 'it's body.' She winked at me. 'Eh, Bolton?'

Lew hadn't seen me listening, and he tried to laugh it off. I didn't take much notice of him. I never do. He's turned fifty, has a thin face with red cheeks and sandy hair. He always wears a big jersey with a polo collar, a check cap, and sandals, and he always has a fag in' his mouth.

Box? You could blow him over. But during the war, with all the shortage of food and fags, he suddenly found himself important, like most little shopkeepers and café owners, and he started giving orders, and took to wearing this boxer's rig-out. I hate fakes and show-offs, and Lew's one. But maybe he's not a bad bloke at heart, for they say he's good for a touch if you're short of cash. But I can never forget that he used to put soda in his tea urn, and I blame that for the guts-ache I used to get. That was before he married Ethel.

I said nothing to Ethel except to give her my usual warm nod and wink, and then I ordered a large tea, and asked could I have some egg and chips.

'Yes,' said Lew. 'She's got the chip pan all ready.'

'I'll bring your tea over,' said Ethel.

I knew he was getting at her over something. And I'd a good idea what it was—a driver called Jackson. Ethel wouldn't shut shop until he'd been. I said nothing because I reckoned I was lucky to get my egg and chips. Practically the only spot in the British Isles you could get them on a Friday night at that hour. I walked across to the big table where Taff and Ned were sitting, and sat at one end.

'I see old Babyface is out on the scout again,' said Taff.

'That dirty little blighter,' said Ned. 'I've known many a speed cop in my day, but never one like him, an' his mate. The way they creep up on your tail and hang there.'

'He's done that man Jackson three times,' said Taff.

'Once more,' said Ned, 'an' his licence will go for a walk for six months.'

Ethel brought my tea. She came up behind me and put it on the table. I saw her brown arm and strong woman's fingers.

Outside a lorry drew on to the parking ground and the

engine revved up and then shut off. Taff said, 'That'll be Jackson.' I could see Lew looking a bit tense.

'It's not Jackson,' said Ethel. She smiled at me, and went back to the counter. The door opened and in came Walter, a driver from St Helens, and behind him his trailer-mate, Willie.

Walter, a short little stiff chap, carrying his lunch basket, and Willie, one of these artistic lads you see around these days, with a silk scarf round his neck. He always followed Walter like a faithful poodle. Walter let out a shout and when he came up to Lew he got up on his toes and began boxing. This just suited Lew who began throwing in what he thought were snappy lefts. Old Walter could have let him have one and knocked him out for good. But he always liked to gee old Lew up a bit. He went up and kissed Ethel on the cheek.

'Love me as much as ever, love?' said Walter to Ethel.

'You know me, Walter,' said Ethel.

'That's why I'm asking,' said Walter.

It was a lively little entrance and it brightened the place up.

Taff called out, 'Did you see old Babyface on your way down?'

'Did we see him, Willie!' said Walter, 'Ethel, double egg and chips for my mate. I'm treating him.' Walter came over to the table and cocked his leg across a chair. 'We were just coming down the Long Hill there, we had the stick out, doing a nice forty-five, and old Willie here crooning away, when he suddenly broke off like he'd been shot. "What's up, Willie?" I says. "Sum'dy on our tail," says Willie. I revved up and put the old stick in and got into gear. I looked through the mirror. Not a thing in sight. I watched closely, not a thing. And I think the lad must be seeing something. I get the old speed down to a bit of a crawl, and still nothing in sight. "Are you sure, Willie," I says. "I am that an' all," says Willie here. Well, I'm crawling along and still can't see nothing, and I comes to thinking that old Willie's psychic bump has let him down. So I tells him to lean out of the cab at his side while I give a chancy swerve and switch off my own lights for better seeing. Right enough it was that Babyface. Him and his mate had been stuck on our tail.'

'What happened then?' said Ned.

'They knew they'd been rumbled,' said Walter. 'So the next thing they drew ahead and went into a side road. And there they're stuck this minute, waiting for the next poor mug that comes down.'

Ethel came across with my egg and chips. A minute later she was back with Willie's.

'Ee, were you expecting me, Ethel?' said Willie, all smiles.

'Not *you*,' said Lew, looking at the door.

I was wiping my plate clean with bread when a lorry came belting off the road on to the parking ground outside. It hammered along and stopped with a loud brake squeal right at the door. Nobody looked up.

'That's Jackson now,' said Willie.

'And a good job his anchors are all right,' said Taff, 'or else——'

'Curse the man,' said Lew. 'He'll drive up to the blasted counter one of these fine days.' He turned what he must have thought was a tough face to the door. We all gave a look that way. It was Jackson all right. Lew quickly dropped his stare and started wiping a table.

'Has he got the rats in him!' said Ned.

'He's not in the best of moods surely,' said Taff.

Jackson came striding up slowly. He had a dark chin, pale face, black hair. As he was passing our table he saw Willie still eating his egg and chips. The sight of the plate seemed to stop him dead. His face went even darker. Willie looked dead nervous. Walter picked up the sauce bottle.

'Here y'are, Willie boy,' he said in a loud easy-going way, 'have a shake of the old bottle.'

Willie smiled at Walter. Jackson went to the next table, an empty one. When Lew saw that Walter had got one over Jackson, he seemed to take heart. He went up to the table. 'What is it?' he said.

'What's what?' said Jackson, looking for Ethel.

'Have you ordered?' said Lew.

'Ordered?' said Jackson. 'I'm not getting measured for a suit. Small tea.'

'That all?' said Lew.

'That an' a bit of peace,' said Jackson.

'You're supposed to bring your own,' said Lew, walking away.

When he went up to the counter I could see he said something to Ethel, and I heard her say: 'There's times when your funny stuff isn't funny, Lew. I'll serve him.'

'You're welcome,' said Lew.

He looked hurt. She took his arm and smiled at him. He smiled back.

'Sorry,' said Ethel.

'We've had eighteen hours of it,' said Lew, looking at the clock. 'Another half-hour and we're through. 'What about a tune?'

Ethel takes the tea across to Jackson. He gives one tight grip over her wrist.

'You want your egg an' chips, don't you, Jack?' she says.
Jackson shakes his head. Lew dropped his coin into the
juke-box, and the next thing you can hear is a woman singing something about 'waltzing with her darling'. It's called
'The Tennessee Waltz'. Jackson kissed Ethel's arm. Then
Ethel moved slowly away from his table, looking like a
woman with a dream on her mind.

As it happens, old Lew is just moving away from the
juke-box, and this music and woman's voice is filling the
place, and Ethel comes up facing Lew with that faraway
walk, and the next thing Lew has got hold of her and is
dancing her gently around to a slow foxtrot or something.

Although I don't like him I had to admit to myself that
he handled it nicely. And he danced nicely too, with a nice
skilful movement. Then all began calling out, 'Life in the
old dog yet', and 'Go on', but there was no doubt they all
liked to see the dance. All except Jackson. His face went
dead poisonous. He kept himself sitting there for a time and
then he got to his feet. He went across to the juke-box, half
turned his back on it, and gave it a back-heeler. It was a
dead sharp kick, and the next thing there was a groan and
the tune died away in the middle of the woman singing
something about 'remembering the night'.

I looked up and saw old Lew's face. One second it had
that look that comes over a chap's face when he's enjoying
a dance. The next it had the look of a child that's had its
dummy snatched out of its mouth in the middle of a good
suck. Ethel gave Jackson a sharp sort of a look and went
behind the counter. Willie looked towards Lew, his big eyes
soft and wide open with sympathy. Lew stood there in a
daze for a couple of ticks, then he went across to Jackson.

'You did that,' he said.

'What about it?' said Jackson.

'You'd no right,' said Lew. 'Didn't you see us dancin'?'

'I saw you,' said Jackson.

'I won't stand for it,' said Lew.

'What'll you do?' said Jackson.

'I'll show you what I'll do,' said Lew. Then he weakened. 'I mean, we were doin' no harm.'

'I told you I wanted some peace,' said Jackson. 'I've had enough din in my ears for the last five hours.'

'But you'd no right,' said Lew. He went across to the juke-box and shook it. You could hear the record whirring round but missing the needle or something. He came hurrying back to Jackson. 'You had no right to do what you did.' he said, talking legal like. 'I'd put my money in that box.'

Jackson leant back in his chair. 'Why didn't you say it was the money was troubling you?' he said. He put his hand in his pocket and drew out a fistful of silver and copper. 'Here y' are,' he said, holding out his hand. 'You can take it outa that.'

Lew, being a money-mean sort of bloke, couldn't help being caught off guard. The sight of money carelessly handled seems to make some people so that they can't think for a minute. He just stared at Jackson and at the money and didn't know what to do. Then Ethel came walking up behind Lew. She went round him in a gentle way, until she was facing Jackson, and before he knew what was happening she brought up her hand with a swift smack under his. The money went right up in the air and flew all over the place.

'And you,' she said, 'can take it out of that!'

Then she turned to Lew like a mother who has gone out into the street to help her lad who is being challenged by a bigger lad. 'Come on, Lew,' she said and led him back to the counter. We drivers said nothing. After all, Jackson himself was a driver. Jackson didn't know where to look or what to do. Then another lorry stopped outside.

The door opened with a quick jerk and in came Clive. A real spiv kid, the clothes, the walk, the lot, even to the old rub of the hands, as though he's going to sell you something. He comes whistling along.

'What you all bloomin' talkin' at once for?' he says, everything being dead silent. 'Large tea, Ethel, two of toast and drip. Don't be tight with the jelly—m'back's bad.'

Clive eyes everybody.

'Howzit goin', Bolton?' he says to me.

'Not bad,' I says.

Suddenly he makes a dive for something on the floor.

'Coo, I'm in bloomin' luck,' he says, picking up half a crown. I beckon with my thumb to where Jackson is sitting. Clive catches on. He goes across and puts it on the table in front of Jackson.

'I wouldn't rob you, Jackson,' he says. 'You might need it. I see old Babyface did you again—back up the road there on the Long Hill.'

As soon as Clive said that, the atmosphere changed.

'Ruddy hard luck, Jackson,' said Ned.

'I hope they don't scrub your licence,' said Taff.

I gave him a look. He didn't seem to have Babyface on his mind. A lot had happened to him since that.

'He must have nailed you just after he left us,' said Walter. He took out his fags, handed them round, hesitated, then held the packet out to Jackson. Jackson thought it over for a moment and then took one. The matey feeling came up then, the feeling of all being drivers and the law always after you.

Clive leant over the table and looked at Jackson. 'I was stuck in a lay-by up the road, mate, when you came whamming past. You was goin' like the clappers of hell. *Whoof*! . . .'

Ethel came up with Clive's tea and toast and drip.

'You was goin' at a hell of a lick, Jackson,' went on Clive. 'What was on your mind?'

Ethel was leaning over the table. I saw Jackson give her a long and hungry look. Ethel looked at him. She picked up his cup. 'Piece of my apple pie?' she said. He nodded. Then he looked at Clive. 'What did you say?' he said.

'Let it pass,' said Clive, his eye following Ethel. He didn't miss much.

The atmosphere had come on matey, and even Lew came up and hung around.

'I wouldn't like to say what I'd do to a cop like that,' said Taff.

'Babyface?' said Lew. 'Got his job to do, ain't he? That's what he's paid for—bookin' you! Well, ain't it?'

'He ain't paid bonus on the job,' said Ned. 'He don't have to creep on your tail. None of the others do it.'

'It's legal, ain't it?' said Lew. 'You keep to the law too, then nob'dy can touch you.'

They went on yapping about the law then, about loads, log sheets, brakes, licences, and all the rest of it, with old Lew sticking his motty in at every chance.

Then Walter said, 'Has it ever struck you, Lew, what a dangerous caper it is—tailing a lorry?'

I saw Jackson suddenly take an interest.

Clive said: 'Suppose you didn't know this geezer was on

your tail? Say you was doin' a nice fifty-five, when you
spotted something just ahead of you?'

'Yeh,' said Ned, 'an' down on the anchors.'

'Pull up with a jerk,' said Clive, 'and where's Babyface?'

'Over the ruddy top,' said Taff.

'No, he ain't,' said Ned, 'he's *under* the back. You get
out an' run round the back, and there's the bogey-men
an' their car, practically buried under the back axle. "Wot
wuz you a-doin of?" says Babyface. So you says, "Testin'
my bloomin' brakes for efficiency. Why, officah, you've
scratched your radiator—not to mention bashin' in your
National 'Ealth dentures!"'

'Come on, Ned,' said Taff, rising, 'you'd talk all night.'

'It's about time you was all off,' said Lew. 'We want to
get to bed.'

Ethel came over with Jackson's tea and apple pie. 'You go
off, Lew,' she said. She looked at Jackson as she put the piece of
pie in front of him, but he was staring down at the table. He
didn't seem to notice the pie, or, come to that, Ethel herself.

'Can I trust you to lock up properly if I go off?' said
Lew to Ethel.

'I'll help her,' said Walter.

'Then I think I'll go off to bed,' said Lew.

'That's right,' said Clive, 'let your brains cool down.
"Keep to the law." Never heard such bull in all my life.'

'Come on, Taff,' said Ned.

They went off.

'I think I'll go,' said Lew.

'All right,' said Walter, 'go, but stop natterin' about it.'

'Don't be long, Ethel,' said Lew. 'Turf 'em out.'

'It's too late to hurry,' said Ethel.

'Good night, Lew,' said Willie.

'Good night, Willie lad,' said Lew.

When Lew had gone off, Clive turned to me: 'Fancy a game of darts, Lofthouse?'

They either call me by the town I come from or its best-known footballer.

'I'm getting down for ten minutes,' I said.

'I'll give you a game, Bermondsey,' said Walter.

They went off, up beside the counter for their darts game. I put my cap on the table and rested my forehead on it, and shut out all the light with my arms. Even if you don't sleep the eyes and head get rested. You need some relief when you've been driving a ten-tonner through the night. Ethel must have come up and sat at Jackson's table, because after a bit I could hear their voices.

'What made you blow your top?' he said.

'I won't stand by and see a young chap taking the micky out of an older one,' she said. 'I don't like you being that way, Jacky.'

'Before I forget,' said Jackson, 'I've something here for you. Hope they're not too squashed. I had to keep 'em out of sight.'

There was a bit of rustling and then Ethel whispered: 'Roses! how lovely, Jacky! Well, I never expected roses!'

Even with my head down I could smell roses.

Ethel must have given him a hand squeeze. He went on: 'Come off with me tonight. I'll wait for you outside in my tub. We'll drive off together. Don't worry about clothes—look, see, I've enough money in that book to buy you all the clothes you want.'

Post Office savings book. But I know how he felt. The

thought of having a woman in the warm cab there beside you, as you drive through the night, is the most tempting thought a driver can get. At least, that I can get. It's so cosy in the cab of your own lorry, with the faint warm smell of diesel oil, but it gets lonely. If only you had a woman beside you. For part of the time anyway.

Ethel went on about Lew: 'When I first came in that door,' I heard her say, 'I wasn't much to look at. I'd had things rough, I can tell you that, Jacky. And Lew is the first man I've ever met who has treated me with respect. He never tried anything on. And that's what I liked about him.'

'Am I trying anything on?' said Jackson. 'I'm asking you to come off with me.'

'And the day we got back after the marriage,' went on Ethel, 'he already had a new sign up outside. It said, "*Lew's and Ethel's*".'

'Come off it,' said Jackson. 'He made the ropiest cup of tea between here and Gretna Green. The place was fallin' apart, an' so was he. You've pulled it all together. You're straight with him.'

'Another thing Lew gave me,' said Ethel, 'was security.'

Jackson seemed to fly off the handle at that. 'Security? What the hell are you talking about! I come bashing down Watling Street tonight—never a perishing stop except to snatch your roses. One thought on my mind—will I see you? How do you think that rat Babyface caught me again? —and you talk to me about security.'

'Sorry, Jacky,' said Ethel. 'What happens if they take your licence?'

'No licence, no job,' said Jackson. 'But we'll see about that. They won't get me working under a roof that easily.'

Just then the juke-box let go 'The Tennessee Waltz' again. I looked up with a start, as though I'd been asleep. Willie was standing beside it. He called across to Walter, 'That's not the record I picked, Walter.' It was just then I looked towards Jackson. He looked real poisonous. He got up and walked slowly towards Willie at the juke-box.

'Jacky!' whispered Ethel. He took no notice.

Walter had spotted him. He left the darts game and hurried casually across to Willie beside the juke-box. Willie had seen Jackson, and he looked white.

'Enjoy yourself, lad,' said Walter. Then he turned and faced Jackson. I got up and walked across. Same as they used to say, Lancashire helps Lancashire. Walter was only a bantam; Jackson was on the big side and tough.

'Move over, Scouse,' said Jackson.

'What d'you want?' said Walter.

'I'm going to stop that ruddy thing,' said Jackson.

'I don't think you are,' said Walter. His eyes never left Jackson as he handed the darts to Willie. I could see what Walter had in mind. He'd grab Jackson's coat lapels in a tick and pull him down and tup him with his head. And Jackson wouldn't be able to see for blood. I could almost hear the crack of Jackson's nose in my ears, even before it happened.

Ethel slipped round.

'What's up?' she said.

'Willie's paid to hear a tune,' said Walter, 'and he's goin' to hear one.'

'Yeh, but it might not be the one he's paid for,' said Jackson.

Jackson had a savage look on his face. But Walter was determined, and on the aware.

'Don't make any trouble,' said Ethel. 'Please go, and let me lock up.'

Jackson turned and looked at her. Walter was ready to make his grab. I stepped in.

'Come on, Walt,' I said.

'Not till the tune's up,' he said.

So we all stood there for half a minute until the woman on the record stopped singing.

'You can all go now,' said Ethel.

'Ee, but we haven't paid yet, Ethel,' said Willie.

'Ee, lad, so you haven't,' said Ethel, taking him off a bit.

That seemed to break up the tension.

'What about the old darts?' said Clive.

Walter took the darts off Willie.

'Is it me?' he said.

'Yip,' said Clive. 'You want seventy-nine for game. Not be a minute, Ethel.'

Walter toed the line. He threw a nineteen, then a twenty, and a double-top with the last dart.

'Who'd 'ave bloomin' thought it!' said Clive, putting down his darts.

We all paid and walked to the door. 'Have you a minute, Bolton?' said Jackson. I nodded. He slipped back and had a last word with Ethel. I went up beside Walter.

'I was right there behind you, Walter,' I said, 'but I reckoned you didn't need me.'

Walter took off his cap and patted his head: 'I had this ready for him,' he said.

I went across to my tub. Then Jackson came up.

'I was going to ask you,' he said; 'you ain't got an old driving mirror, have you?'

As soon as he said it I remembered I had one in my tool-box. And it struck me that he must have seen it when I once lent him a spanner. He took out his fags and handed me one. Then he shone the torch in my tool-box. I got the driving mirror out. It was one that had been wrenched away when I drew too close to a wagon at the sidings one day. The metal arm had been ripped from the bracket.

'That do you?' I said.

'It might,' he said.

I didn't ask him what he wanted it for. If he wants me to know, I reckoned, he'll tell me.

'You've been done for speeding?' he said.

'More'n once,' I said.

'The cop who charges you has got to have a witness—that so?' he said.

'His mate,' I said, 'that's all.'

'There's got to be two of 'em in court,' he said.

'If you plead "not guilty" an' make a case of it,' I said. 'But how many drivers do? You know damn' well you're guilty.'

'But they've *both* got to be there,' he said. 'Haven't they?'

'Look here, Jackson,' I said, 'if you're goin' on about Babyface doin' you tonight, forget it. You——'

'Look here,' cut in Jackson, 'if you want to question his witness and his witness fails to appear, or either one of them fails to appear——'

'Then it's "failure to produce witnesses",' I said, 'and you get "Case Dismissed".'

'That's what I wanted to know,' said Jackson.

'But I'll tell you one thing you're sufferin' from, Jackson,' I said, 'that's a bad dose of *copitis*.'

'You said it,' he said. 'I could murder the perishing lot of 'em.'

'It won't get you nowhere,' I said. 'We've all had it some time or other. Anyway, they won't take your licence just for speedin'.'

'It's not speedin'. He's doin' me for dangerous drivin',' said Jackson.

'That's a bit more serious,' I said.

'An' not only that,' said Jackson.

'What else?' I said.

'I'd a fiver folded up in my licence when I handed it over,' he said.

'A fiver! You must be crazy,' I said. 'It should be a quid. An' you get the licence back with a caution an' no quid. What's wrong with that? I'd sooner give a cop a quid than a magistrate a fiver.'

'I'd sooner cut their throats,' said Jackson, 'the lot of 'em. Babyface is trying to make out I wanted to bribe him.'

'I suppose you said you kept it in your licence for safety?' I said.

Jackson nodded.

'Then,' I said, 'it's your word against his.'

'Against his and his mate's, and I know whose they'll take,' he said. Then he picked up the mirror and had a good look at it. 'We'll see,' he said. 'They ain't heard the charge yet. There's another three weeks to go. Anything could happen in that time.' He waved the mirror and went off.

It was a fortnight later, about two o'clock in the morning, a pitch black night, and I was belting along Watling Street, hoping I might make 'Lew's' in time. I was going at a fair lick, because you can see better on a dark night, since your headlights carve out the road for you, and you don't get those dicey shadows the moon makes. I had my eye watching out for Babyface, for I knew I was on his beat.

Suddenly, ahead down the road, I saw a lorry's headlights flashing on and off, giving me the danger signal. I flashed back, braked, and watched the road behind me and the road ahead. You can't be too careful on a trunk road at night.

I drew up in a safe clear spot. In the beam of my headlight I could see a lorry skew-whiff across the road. There was a black car that had crashed into the back of it with such force that it seemed to be buried under the chassis. I lit a fag. As I was getting out a driver came running up to me.

'Leave your headlights on, Bolton,' he called. 'They need all the light they can get.'

'That you, Ned?' I said. 'What's happened?'

'A right smash-up,' said Ned. He whispered: 'It's old Jackson. Police car run into the back of him. They're trying to get the bodies out.'

We walked down together to the smash-up. The police and ambulance men were on the job. They were trying to jack up the back axle of the lorry so that they could get the car out. The police car hooter was going all the time. The blue plate on the back of the car with the word 'POLICE' on it was intact, but that was about all that was. Nobody would ever drive that car again. As for the two blokes inside, well, one glimpse was enough.

'Babyface?' I said to Ned.

'It was,' said Ned. 'The poor blighter. His mate, too.' He gave me a knowing look, but said no more.

I heard someone talking in a husky voice and I turned and saw Jackson. He was talking to a young patrol cop who was making notes in his book.

'Well, I'll tell you all I know,' said Jackson. 'I'm coming along at a fair crack. No use wrapping it up, I had my toe down, because I wanted to get to the caff down the road before they close. I usually have egg and chips about this time. But I was keeping my eyes open and the road was dead clear in front of and behind me—so far as I could see. I could have sworn to it. And I was just coming along there, when on the bend here, dead in front of me, I saw what looked like a body curled in the roadway.'

'A body?' said the cop. 'Where is it now?'

'I looked after,' said Jackson. 'See—under there.'

He pointed under his lorry. We all looked.

'That old overcoat?' said the cop.

'I can see what it is *now*,' said Jackson. 'But catch it in your headlights an' it looks different.'

The cop nodded.

'I've known many an old geezer get drunk and go to sleep in the middle of the road,' went on Jackson. 'Anyway, I slammed on my brakes at once. Then I got the shock of my life. *Something hit me from behind.* I couldn't think what had happened. It wasn't a tap, it was a real bash. Even with my brakes on it knocked me across the road.'

The patrol cop looked sympathetic.

'What did you do then?' he asked.

'It took me a minute or two to come round,' said Jackson. 'The shock and one thing and another. Then I got out of the cab and walked round to the back. It's dark, see, and for a bit I couldn't make out what had happened. I could hear his horn blowing away in my ears, but I didn't know where it was coming from, not at first. Then suddenly I began to make it out. I looked inside the car and saw 'em. It was a shock, mate, I can tell you that. How are they? Will they be all right?'

'Take it easy,' said the cop. 'We're doing all we can.'

Jackson wiped his face with his hand: 'Is it all right if I walk down the road and get myself a cup of tea?' he asked. 'I feel all out.'

The cop said, 'Just a minute, I'll see.' He went up to a police sergeant and one of the ambulance men. Jackson turned and winked at me, then he went on wiping his forehead. The patrol cop came back and said, 'So long as you are not too far away.'

Jackson said, 'I'll be in the caff.'

'Better let me have your licence,' said the cop.

'I'll get it out of my coat pocket,' said Jackson, 'in the cab. He turned to me. 'You'll give me a lift down the road, Lofty?'

The cop warmed up: 'Come on,' he said, 'let's get the road clear, or we'll be having another smash-up. Tell the other drivers not to line up along there.'

Jackson got into my cab. I drove round by his lorry and down the road to 'Lew's'. He was thinking about something and he said nothing as we went down the road, and I didn't feel like talking either. When I drew up to a halt outside Lew's he turned to me and digging his hand inside his coat he carefully pulled something out.

' 'Ere you are, mate,' he said.

I looked. In his hand was the driving mirror I had lent him. The glass was broken.

'It came in handy,' he said.

I didn't say anything. He looked like a man at peace with himself.

'I had it planted down below the floorboards,' he said.

'Oh, aye?' I said.

I wasn't as surprised as I made it sound.

'It was there waiting for Babyface,' he said. 'I knew whenever he crept on my tail, even if he had all his lights out, I'd spot him down in that mirror. Half an hour ago I caught him creeping up behind me. Right, I thought to myself, I'll draw you on, Charlie. I stuck in the booster gear and put my toe down. They fell for it and crept right up behind me. I was coming down Long Hill and I knew the exact spot he'd overtake me, just near the bend at the bottom. So as we were drawing near to it I got every ounce I could out of the old tub. We were fair cracking along, I can tell you. *Right mate*, I thought, *you're trying to do me, but I'm going to do you instead*. So, I steeled myself for the shock, then I slammed both feet down at once and swung on the handbrake at the same time.'

Jackson scratched his nose: 'I've got some lovely ancnors on the old wagon. They drew me up like that. They'd have had to be good drivers to stop that quick. They didn't have a chance. They crashed right clean in the back.'

I felt I needed a bit of fresh air after that lot, so I got out of the cab. Jackson got out at the other side and walked round to me.

'First thing I did, when I stopped,' he said, 'was to take that old mirror out and put the floorboard back straight. Breaking that mirror brought 'em bad luck all right. Then I took that old topcoat that I had specially for the job and planted it on the road under the lorry. It's not mine.'

He followed me round as I kicked at my tyres, and tested my loading ropes.

'Well, here's your mirror, mate,' he said.

I could hardly bear to look at it, let alone take hold of it.

'If you don't want it, I can soon lose it for you,' said Jackson. He was back in a minute. 'Take a ruddy good detective to find it now,' he said.

'Jackson,' I said, 'what's the idea telling me all this?'

He smiled softly at me and then he said: 'A bloke don't want to walk round with a basinful of that on his mind. I know I'm safe with an old driver. Come on, let's see if Ethel has the egg and chips ready.'

I followed him. At the door he turned and said to me: 'Nothing I like better than getting one across the law. Y'know what it means for my dangerous drivin' charge?— *Case dismissed.*'

I went in after him. There were half a dozen drivers in. Walter and Willie, young Clive, a driver and his mate from Glasgow, and an old driver from Hull. They all gave nods and waves to me. But as for Jackson, not a word was spoken. Not a sign was made. You felt everything going dead quiet. Lew was wiping the tables and kept right away from where Jackson sat. Ethel was behind the counter and she never gave him so much as a glance. She looked across to me and waved her hand. Jackson looked at her, but she didn't seem to see him. I knew then the word had gone round. It doesn't take long. He might have got one across the law, but he hadn't got one across Watling Street. Nobody would split, but already, North and South, they were putting the poison in for him. Within a week, he'd be lucky to get a civil cup of tea anywhere along the A5. And I could see by the look on Jackson's face he knew one thing at least —no matter what the police found or didn't find—he'd never get anywhere with Ethel now. And his driving days on Watling Street were over.

QUESTIONS FOR DISCUSSION ONLY

The First Seven Years (page 11)

1. Why does Feld want Miriam to have a good education?

2. Why was Feld disappointed to find that Max was studying accountancy?

3. Why did Feld arrange for Max to go out with Miriam? Was there more than one reason?

4. What did Miriam mean when she said that Max 'has no soul. He's only interested in things'? (p. 20)

5. Which of the characters seem to you to be educated people and which not?

6. Do you think that Max would have made a better husband than Sobel?

7. 'Then he realized that what he had called ugly was not Sobel but Miriam's life if she married him.' (p. 24) Why should Sobel think that this life would be ugly? Do you agree?

Shot Actress—Full Story (page 25)

1. 'No one in Claypole knew much about Miss Porteus.' (p. 25) Why not?

2. What made Sprake climb to Miss Porteus's bathroom window?

3. Should Sprake have climbed the ladder to be photographed?

4. Which of the things that Sprake told to the photographers were they interested in? Why did they choose these?

5. 'There sprang up, gradually, a different story about Miss Porteus.' (p. 32) Why, do you think, did people make this up? Why did they start ugly stories about Sprake?

6. Whose fault was the death of Mrs Sprake and the failure of the shop? Was it the newspapermen's?

7. What kind of a person was Sprake?

The Little Pet (page 38)

1. What sort of people were the parents? How did they behave to their son?

2. Why do they talk about the rabbit in the way that they do?

3. 'A darling of a bunny brer-rabbit.' (p. 40) In what ways does the description of the actual rabbit give a different impression from this?

4. What changes do you notice during the story in the way that they treat the rabbit? Why is this?

5. Why, do you think, does the boy know of the killing of the baby rabbit before his parents do?

6. Why does this story end with 'I'm not cross with you. I knew you didn't like your baby'? (p. 47) How did the boy know?

7. Is this merely a story about the death of a baby rabbit? Why, then, does it give an impression not merely of sadness but of tragedy? Or do you find signs of hope in it?

8. What is the point of its title?

Life of Ma Parker (page 48)

1. 'I hope the funeral went off all right.' (p. 48) 'It must be rather nice to be married to a baker.' (p. 52) Look at these and the other things that the literary gentleman says

to and about Ma Parker. What can you learn about him from them?

2. 'Lennie gone—what had she? She had nothing.' (p. 55) Why did she feel this about Lennie's death? Do you think she usually felt so sorry for herself?

3. Why had Ma Parker never cried? Why couldn't she cry now? Why would it help her if she could?

4. Why does the story end with 'There was nowhere'? Does it make you feel sad or angry?

A Message from the Pig-Man (page 57)

1. What things were worrying Ekky?

2. Why had he such wrong ideas about the Pig-man?

3. How did he get rid of his fears of the Pig-man? What did he learn from this? Was it true?

4. Why did Ekky decide 'that grown-ups were mad and silly'? (p. 65) Do you think that he was very upset?

5. Should his mother have answered his question differently? What could she have said?

6. Why bring the Pig-man into the story at all? Was Ekky really so very frightened of him?

The Dry Rock (page 66)

1. Pidgear said: 'This whole affair is niggling'. (p. 75) Do you think that Tarloff was right to call in the police about it?

2. What would you guess about Rusk and the four men in grey hats? Why was Rusk so eager not to be charged?

3. What sort of person was Rusk? Do you think it important for him to be punished?

4. Why was Helen so unsympathetic to Tarloff? What sort of thing did she seem to care about?

5. Why did Tarloff refuse the money and the farc at the end?

6. Whose fault was it that Rusk wasn't punished? Tarloff's? Do you think that Fitzsimmons did all he could?

Through the Tunnel (page 81)

1. 'She was determined to be neither possessive nor lacking in devotion.' (p. 82) What things that the mother did or said would have told us this even if the author had not?

2. Did Jerry merely long to get away from his mother, or did he find it hard to decide what he wanted?

3. Why did the author choose to put the tunnel in a different bay from that in which Jerry's mother sat?

4. When Jerry first tried he could not even find the tunnel, but a fortnight later he was able to swim through it. What things had changed during that fortnight?

5. 'He could see the local boys diving and playing half a mile away. He did not want them. He wanted nothing but to get back home and lie down.' (p. 92) Does the last sentence completely explain why he did not want the local boys? Can you suggest another reason?

6. His mother wasn't very excited when he told her how long he spent underwater. Why, do you think, did this not matter to him?

7. Why, in your opinion, did he so much want to swim through the tunnel?

A Present for a Good Girl (page 94)

1. What did the shop assistants think about the old woman when she first came into the shop? Judging from the description of her appearance, do you think that they were right?

2. If you had been the assistant would you have let her reserve the bag?

3. 'Underneath her stiff face, her glassed-out eyes, it was horrible to see that she was alive and struggling.' (p. 104) When the old woman is drunk, do *you* find her horrible? Or funny, or pitiful, or something else?

4. Why did the old woman want to buy the expensive bag for her daughter? And why did she fail to pay the money?

5. Why was her daughter angry instead of being grateful? How would you have felt in her place?

6. ' "Come on," she ordered in a low dead voice.' (p. 105) All the girl's anger seemed to have gone. Can you explain this? What did she feel in the place of anger?

Possessions (page 106)

1. Why was it the piano and the pony that Ma fought to keep?

2. 'None of us wanted to part with him.' (p. 106) Why then did they sell the pony?

3. Had Ma any right to tell Dando off about how he looked after the pony once he had bought it? Didn't they really steal the pony when they took it back?

4. 'Gomer can learn the flute.' (p. 116) Why were they now more ready to let the piano go?

5. Why was Dando willing to take the old piano in place of the pony?

6. At the end Ma said, 'I wonder how the piano is getting on.' What does this tell us about Ma and her possessions?

The Raid (page 120)

1. Dick said that Root was scared about the meeting. Was there something that Root was even more scared of?

2. Root's words about his father (p. 121) suggest that he was young. What else do these words show?

3. What else is there in the story to show that he was unsure of himself?

4. Why did they not run away? Were they foolish not to? What would you have done?

5. 'Remember about it's not them, it's the System.' (p. 131) What did Dick mean?

6. Do you think they should have fought back? Why didn't they?

7. Was Root right when he said, 'But there wasn't no religion to it'? (p. 133) Why did these words come to him? How are they appropriate?

8. The meeting was a political one. Do you think that there is any point in a small group of people risking their lives for politics?

The Living (page 134)

1. What differences do you notice between Mickser and the boy who tells the story? Does this seem to be connected with the way that each has been brought up by his parents? How do their feelings about dead people seem to differ?

2. 'They'll be glad to see us.' (p. 138) Notice Mickser's account of the welcome for visitors to the wake. Do you

think that this is a right way of behaving when someone in the family has died?

3. Why did Mickser run away? Did the story-teller run away for the same reason?

4. 'Isn't it better God took him before yourself, anyway?' (p. 142) Why did the other woman think this?

5. The widow replied: 'And what if I do forget? I'll have nothing at all then!' (p. 143) What did she mean? What didn't she want to forget?

6. Why was the widow so glad that the boys wanted to see her husband?

7. How can you tell that the boy's family was a happy one? Who seemed to do most to make it happy?

8. What had happened a moment before to make the boy, in the midst of his family, feel that 'the living and the dead' were 'terrible words'? (p. 149) What difference had the visit to the dead man made to him?

9. Why does the story end with 'For a long time'?

10. Is this a morbid story? ('Morbid' means 'taking an unhealthy interest in death.)'

Uncle Ernest (page 150)

1. 'No pink scar marked his flesh from shellshock and a jolted brain.' (p. 153). But how did his experiences during the war affect him?

2. What made Ernest buy food for the girls? What kind of satisfaction did it bring him?

3. Were the presents and the food he bought doing them any harm? Did their behaviour to him change at all?

4. Do you think that the police were right to treat Ernest as they did?

5. Why did Ernest panic when he was forbidden to see the girls again?

Late Night on Watling Street (page 164)

1. Would you have disliked Jackson even if he hadn't killed the policeman?

2. What do you think of the other lorry-drivers in this story? Would you like to be one of the crowd that meets in Lew's café?

3. Bolton says, 'I hate fakes and show-offs, and Lew's one.' (p. 165) Do you agree with Bolton about Lew, or has he good points?

4. What reasons does Ethel give Jackson for not going away with him? Does she love Lew? Why did she knock the money out of Jackson's hand? (p. 170)

5. Why does the writer bring the affair between Ethel and Jackson into the story? Does he imply that it was wrong?

6. How do the drivers feel about the police? Have they any good reason for this? Why does Ned say of Babyface, 'He ain't paid bonus on the job'? (p. 172).

7. Why is it particularly important to Jackson that he is not taken to court just at this time? Does this at all alter the way you feel about his crime?

8. If you were acting Jackson in a dramatized version of this story how would you say the part (p. 183) where he tells Bolton how he did the murder?

9. Jackson said, 'I know I'm safe with an old driver.' (p. 184) How 'safe' was he? Why didn't the drivers report the crime to the police? Should they have done? What was Jackson's punishment? Is this a proper way of doing justice?